BEHOLDEN

THE FAIREST MAIDENS
ONE

Books by Jody Hedlund

Young Adult: The Fairest Maidens Series
Beholden
Beguiled
Besotted

Young Adult: The Lost Princesses Series
Always: Prequel Novella
Evermore
Foremost
Hereafter

Young Adult: The Noble Knights Series
The Vow: Prequel Novella
An Uncertain Choice
A Daring Sacrifice
For Love & Honor
A Loyal Heart
A Worthy Rebel

The Bride Ships Series
A Reluctant Bride
The Runaway Bride
A Bride of Convenience
Almost a Bride

The Orphan Train Series
An Awakened Heart: A Novella
With You Always
Together Forever
Searching for You

The Beacons of Hope Series
Out of the Storm: A Novella
Love Unexpected
Hearts Made Whole
Undaunted Hope
Forever Safe
Never Forget

The Hearts of Faith Collection
The Preacher's Bride
The Doctor's Lady
Rebellious Heart

The Michigan Brides Collection
Unending Devotion
A Noble Groom
Captured by Love

Historical
Luther and Katharina
Newton & Polly

BEHOLDEN

THE FAIREST MAIDENS
ONE

JODY HEDLUND

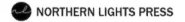

NORTHERN LIGHTS PRESS

Beholden
Northern Lights Press
© 2020 Copyright
by Jody Hedlund
Jody Hedlund Print Edition

ISBN 978-1-7337534-5-6

www.jodyhedlund.com

Scripture quotations are taken from the King James Version of the Bible.

This is a work of historical reconstruction; the appearances of certain historical figures are accordingly inevitable. All other characters are products of the author's imagination. Any resemblance to actual events or locales or persons, living or dead, is entirely coincidental.

Cover Design by Roseanna White Designs
Interior Map Design by Jenna Hedlund

Chapter 1

VILMAR

I KNELT BEFORE MY FATHER, KING CHRISTIAN. MY TWO BROTHERS did likewise on either side of me.

"The time for the Testing has come." The king's voice resounded through the great hall, which was filled to overflowing with nobility and commoners alike, vying to witness the fate of their princes.

"We are ready, Your Majesty," I said in unison with my brothers, our heads bent low.

Though I spoke the words expected of me, a part of me questioned whether I needed the Royal Testing. After all, of the three of us, I already had the favor of the Lagting. In fact, 'twas no secret the king's council would likely pick me to inherit the throne.

The clanking of a sword against Mikkel's chain mail to my left signaled the beginning of the ritual. As firstborn, Mikkel had the privilege of going first in many things. But birth order was no guarantee of kingship. Not in Scania, where each prince had to prove himself through the Testing in order to be chosen as the successor.

I slid a glance sideways, catching sight of the gleaming weapon resting upon Mikkel's shoulder. The sword was magnificent with its double-edged blade and the hilt inlaid with a striking zigzag pattern of silver and copper.

"After much forethought"—the king held the sword steady on Mikkel's shoulder—"the Lagting has decided that you, Prince Mikkel, shall seek your Testing in Norland on the Isle of Outcasts."

Norland? We had speculated for months where the Lagting would send us. We should have guessed they would choose the three countries on the Great Isle, since our mother, Queen Joanna, had hailed from there. As the youngest sister of Alfred the Peacemaker, one of the greatest kings the Great Isle had ever known, our mother often spoke of her homeland with fondness.

The king lifted the sword and touched Mikkel's other shoulder. "You must seek to live out the ancient wisdom that says: *Look on the heart.*" The words were engraved with detailed craftsmanship into the sword's blade and would serve as a reminder of the challenge Mikkel had been given. Of course, he must uncover the deeper meaning and how it pertained to him specifically. But that was all part of the Testing.

"I accept the Testing." Mikkel's solemn voice filled the silence. "And I shall endeavor to complete it with my body, soul, and spirit."

King Christian removed the sword and stepped back. The bishop, with a dangling silver thurible, took his place in front of Mikkel and chanted the words of an ancient prayer. Smoky incense billowed from the thurible as the bishop swung it back and forth, letting the sweet waft of myrrh cover Mikkel and rise toward heaven.

My older brother would indeed need much prayer.

The Isle of Outcasts was fraught with much danger from warring bands of criminals and misfits who lived there. I did not envy the place he must go.

"Rise, Prince Mikkel," the king said once the prayer was complete. Mikkel stood and the sunlight streaming in from the high open window touched upon my brother's fair hair, which he'd left unbound for the occasion. It hung just past his shoulders in gentle waves, freshly washed and well-groomed, with a single thin braid the only decoration.

I'd styled mine in a similar fashion. While Mikkel's hair color was like golden barley, Kresten and I shared the same rich, earthy brown of a fallow field. Having slightly differing builds and brawn, we all bore our father's blue eyes, rugged countenance, and broad frame.

I was not deaf to the flattery that flowed through the royal court regarding how handsome we three brothers were. Nor was I blind to the admiration bestowed upon us by many young maidens. And yet, as much as I thrived on such attention and had even relished the company of pretty damsels, I'd never pursued a serious relationship—not when the king and the Lagting were in the process of securing advantageous matches.

The time would be right for love and marriage once we'd passed the Testing and learned which of us would become the next king. Only then would Father and the Lagting finish making the arrangements.

As the king handed Mikkel his new, prized sword and then kissed both his cheeks, I braced myself for my commissioning. Where would the Lagting send me? And what would my challenge be?

Their private deliberations had been ongoing for months. And now that the spring thaw had melted the dangerous ice floes that wrecked many an unsuspecting fishing boat or merchant vessel, we could emerge from our winter hibernation. Mikkel, Kresten, and I would have no trouble traveling to any destination chosen for us.

The king took his place in front of me, and I bowed my head lower, paying this great man homage. He was indeed proof that the Testing served its purpose in showing which prince deserved the title and responsibility of being king of Scania. He and his brothers had gone through the Testing over twenty-five years ago, and the Lagting had chosen Christian as being most worthy of the kingship. Like me, he'd also been the middle of three sons.

The heavy weight of a blade descended upon my shoulder. At the contact of my new, coveted sword, I closed my eyes and whispered a prayer of my own—a prayer for blessing and success in the days to come.

"After much forethought"—the king repeated the words of the ritual—"the Lagting has decided that you, Prince Vilmar, will seek your Testing in Warwick in the mine pits of the Gemstone Mountains."

The mine pits of the Gemstone Mountains. My mind spun with all I'd ever learned about the gem mines. Located in central Warwick, the Gemstone Mountain Range had been so named when emeralds, rubies, sapphires, and diamonds had been discovered there during the reign of King Alfred the Peacemaker.

The abundance of jewels had made Warwick a valuable and rich land, one King Alfred had bestowed upon Margery, the older of his twin daughters. He'd given Mercia to the other twin, Leandra, dividing the once-united Bryttania into two smaller kingdoms. The sisters had ruled their kingdoms peacefully for several years until Leandra died giving birth to her firstborn child, Aurora.

Upon Leandra's death, Margery had insisted that Mercia belonged to her, that she had more right to be queen there than Leandra's babe. Margery wanted to reunite and rule all of Bryttania the way her father had.

Thus began many years of Queen Margery searching for the infant in order to kill her. If the rumors were true, Queen Margery hadn't yet found Aurora, who'd lived in hiding all these years. While I was related to Queen Margery, since she was my mother's niece, I'd never met her before, and after what I'd heard, I also had no desire for introductions.

My father lifted the sword from my left shoulder and brought it down onto my right. "You must seek to live out the ancient wisdom that says: *Be slave of all.*"

Slave? Indeed, indeed. Since I must journey into the mines of the Gemstone Mountains, it followed that I must learn to live as a slave. While most of the range had been cleared of gems long ago, apparently new jewels were still being discovered but were deeper and harder to excavate with every passing year. The work was so dangerous and difficult only slaves could be persuaded to go inside and retrieve the precious gems.

Certainly, no matter the difficulty, I could accomplish such a task for the six months the Testing required.

"I accept the Testing," I said in a clear voice that projected to the people crowded into the great hall and rose into the high arched ceiling. "I shall endeavor to complete it with my body, soul, and spirit."

The bishop took his turn praying and spreading the thurible's fragrant incense over me. Then, upon my father's command, I stood and received my new sword, reading the bold engraving on the blade: *Be slave of all.*

The king repeated the Testing commission for

Kresten. All the while, from the corner of my eye, I assessed the stately group of men standing at the right hand of the king's throne, attired in their long white robes trimmed with lynx and fox fur. The council was composed of officials who represented the thirteen most populated districts in Scania. Many of them were older than the king, having been chosen to be on the Lagting long ago in ceremonies similar to those required of the princes.

I'd known the council members my whole life, but only within recent years had I taken the time to seek them out individually and learn under them with the hope I would grow in my own wisdom.

Why had they chosen slavery for me? I guessed there was a profound purpose, that the meaning was just as cryptic as Mikkel's engraving. Whatever the case, I vowed to complete my challenge to the best of my ability.

As Kresten received his Testing, I wasn't surprised to discover he would have to go to the Great Isle too. He was tasked with living in Mercia's Inglewood Forest as a woodcutter, and the engraving on his new sword stated: *Deny Thyself.*

After the last prayer of the ceremony, the gathering erupted into cheering and clapping. My brothers and I hugged and backslapped each other. Then we took our places at the head table with the king and queen for a final feast that would last well into the night, ushering in the first day of May. We would not get much sleep before our ship set sail for the Great Isle, but I didn't mind. I would gladly relinquish slumber for the chance to say farewell to friends and have one last night of entertainment before the months of toil and deprivation.

After we finished eating, I pushed back from the head table and stood. "I would like to make a toast." Empty platters and trenchers spread out before us, the mutton picked clean, the greasy bones all that remained of the meal.

I lifted my chalice of spiced mead. The laughter and talking tapered to silence, leaving only the crackling of the large hearth fire at the center of the hall. Though the room was dimly lit and hazy with smoke, I could still see the approval and love on the dozens of faces directed my way. Friends, fellow knights, and the most important men in the country. Already they saw me as their future ruler. The Testing would confirm it.

"My dear countrymen," I said once all eyes were upon me. "On the eve of the Testing, we want you to know that we willingly go out into the world and place ourselves in the severest circumstances in order to prove our worthiness to you."

I glanced to Mikkel on one side of me and Kresten on the other, and they both nodded their agreement. Mikkel's features radiated somberness. As usual, he'd likely taken more time to ponder the dangers and difficulties we would encounter in the days to come. Kresten, on the other hand, boasted a wide grin, eager for the challenges and adventures.

While we three princes were decidedly distinct, we each shared many characteristics forged during the rigorous training and education we'd been given in our childhood and youth. Most importantly, the king and queen had instilled the value of our brotherly bonds, that our friendship with each other must supersede any claim for the throne.

In truth, I could say that even if I lost the Testing, I'd harbor no bitterness or ill will toward my brothers. While I might be disappointed in myself, I admired them and would serve underneath them if that's what the Lagting decided. And they felt the same about me, although of late, I'd sensed more tension with Mikkel.

I lifted my chalice first toward Mikkel and then Kresten. "I wish the best for each of my brothers. May God grant you wisdom and strength in the days to come."

They lifted their chalices in return before we sipped. Then I raised my cup toward my father and mother sitting at the center of the table. "I wish for the king and queen long life. May God grant you many more happy days."

My father nodded his acceptance and my mother smiled, her eyes radiating her pride in my brothers and me. In her snow-white gown, with the traditional Scania headdress covering her long blond hair, Queen Joanna was exquisite. Crystal beads and jewels dangled from the circlet around her head and made a tinkling sound every time she turned. The Great Isle was known for its beautiful women, and she was no exception.

"Finally, to all the citizens of Scania." I shifted my chalice toward the long room and the full tables. "We pledge our loyalty, our love, and our lives to you."

After a chorus of affirmation, I drank from the cup and envisioned myself as king one day, standing in this spot in the great hall and drinking another toast to the peace and security of the country and people I cherished.

When the last of the guests had fallen asleep on benches or stretched out in the rushes on the floor, I allowed myself to rest for an hour before I rose and retired to my chamber. After grooming with the help of my manservant, I strapped on my new sword alongside my seax. The curved knife was my weapon of choice, since I'd long ago perfected its use. While I'd have to leave my sword behind once I was bound as a slave in the mines, the seax I could easily sneak inside, concealing it in the hiding place in the thick sole of my boot.

Still sated from the feasting of the night, I didn't waste time breaking my fast. Instead, I spent my last hour amongst my closest friends and servants, saying my farewells. As they accompanied me down the mountain, the light of dawn broke over the eastern crags. I drew in a deep breath of the frigid spring air thick with brine and allowed myself a moment to appreciate the landscape.

Bergenborg Castle had been built two centuries ago on the high bluff overlooking the fjord. Thus, it provided not only a strategic advantage against anyone daring enough to attack, but it afforded the most stunning view in all of Scania. The inlet's deep-blue mouth was calm and glassy, reflecting the tall cliffs on either side. The recently thawed waterfalls on the north side cascaded down the steep rock face.

Towering in the distance beyond the cliffs, the mountain ranges were still covered in thick layers of snow and ice that would linger well into the summer, but whose runoff would eventually turn the rivers and fjords even clearer and bluer. The evergreens somehow managed to find places to grow here and there amongst the jutting rocks, with clumps of pine and spruce interspersed with scrub consisting of dwarf birch, juniper, and all varieties of willow bushes.

No doubt Mikkel had spent his last hour walking the trails that led out onto the cliffs. As I scanned the surrounding area, I half-expected to see him standing tall and proud on a nearby outcropping. But if he was out admiring the beauty of our homeland one last time, I didn't see him.

Kresten, on the other hand, had already arrived at the waterfront. He stood on the wharf talking with several sailors, clearly eager to be on his way. If the weather cooperated, we would have several days and nights of hard rowing before we reached the Great Isle. If we were able to catch the wind, we might be able to raise our sails and make better time. But with the unpredictability of the East Sea during the spring, we could take no risks.

As my companions and I descended the trail, their cajoling and friendly banter kept me from thinking too gravely on my imminent departure. At this early hour, the streets were mostly deserted. The fishermen had already departed for the day in their boats, determined to catch their fill of the salmon, cod, and pollack that entered the fjords during the spring. A few tradesmen had begun the process of opening their shops, and the scent of smoked salmon permeated the air.

Upon reaching the longboat, I tossed my pack inside. It would serve as my seat whenever I rowed. Oars were at the ready, spaced evenly apart throughout the shallow hull. The small vessel needed a crew of eighteen, with nine men on either side. While I was accustomed to the larger royal longships, I understood the practicality of arriving at the Great Isle with anonymity, since we didn't want to draw undue attention to ourselves and the fact we were princes. The Testing rules didn't prohibit disclosing our true identities, but such a revelation could interfere with the end results.

The sun had crested the peaks by the time Mikkel made his way down the winding castle pathway. I was surprised to see that a dozen or more men accompanied him, including the king.

As I watched Mikkel converse with our father, unease chilled my skin as surely as the mist blowing off the fjord. I should have waited and walked with the king to the waterfront. I could have used the hour to solidify our relationship and maintain his goodwill.

When the entourage reached the wharf, the king embraced Mikkel. I could only watch with growing trepidation. Had Mikkel done more to earn our father's and the Lagting's favor than I'd realized?

As my older brother stepped away from Father and crossed toward me, something in his eyes seemed to challenge me—a glint that left no doubt he wanted to become the next king every bit as much as I did and that he would fight me to win the Testing.

Rather than challenging him in return, I gave him one of my usual easy grins. "Are you ready, my brother?" I summoned all the warmth and kindness I could muster.

"As ready as can be. You?"

"I would have another week or month or year before setting out."

Mikkel didn't smile in return. "Perhaps you would like to gain permission to be excused from the Testing?"

My grin slipped away. "I cannot abide any conflict between us, Mikkel. I would rather be excused from the Testing and give up any chance at being king than allow the quest to drive us asunder."

Mikkel held my gaze for several heartbeats before he shifted his attention to the longboat and the sailor on the mast securing the rigging. "Forgive me for my impertinence. In the days to come, we must not lose sight of our affinity for each other. It is the Testing itself that will determine who is most worthy, and as such, we must accept the outcome."

He was right. The Testing was the fairest way to determine our worthiness. We would have no squabbling or fighting or backstabbing between us. Rather than competing against each other, we would be competing against ourselves—our own weaknesses, our own struggles, and our own vulnerabilities.

"I pray Providence will smile upon you with your Testing," I said. "You are a strong and determined man, and you will do well."

This time when Mikkel met my gaze, the ice was gone. "Thank you. You are a good man, Vilmar. And I wish you all the best as well."

Before we could say more, Father's weapons master, Sir Axel, stepped forward and cleared his throat. He was a tall, bald man with a pointed black goatee. The scar running the length of his jaw lent him a fierceness that, in my childhood, had caused me to quake at his appearance. But after years of training under him, I'd ascertained he was not as hard on the inside as he was on the outside.

For several minutes, he relayed the rules of the Testing we'd already learned but that needed restating so no one could claim ignorance. "As always, the Testing involves many risks," he finished in his deep, gravelly voice. "And this will likely involve greater risks than previous Testings due to the volatile situation on the Great Isle."

"Volatile?" Kresten stood beside me with his feet spread and his arms crossed. He was slightly smaller than me, but he was undoubtedly the strongest of the three of us.

"Aye, Queen Margery can be quite unpredictable. If

she discovers any of you on the Isle, there is no telling what she'll do to you." Sir Axel spoke to all of us, but he looked directly at me, since my Testing would be in the heart of her country.

I returned his gaze just as frankly. "Scania is at peace with Warwick. The queen has no grievance with us."

"She doesn't need a grievance. Your presence alone will be enough to raise her suspicion. If she learns of you, she may accuse you of spying or attempting to steal her precious gems. She won't hesitate to fabricate lies to serve her own scheming."

I had faith I could remain undetected in the gem mines. If the queen somehow discovered my presence, I would have to win her over like I did most people I met.

The king raised his hand, his many rings gleaming in the morning light. Sir Axel took the cue and bowed his head. "Your Majesty."

"Please tread carefully, my sons." The king's serious gaze alighted upon each of us. "For if you do find yourself in conflict with Queen Margery, you know the rules of the Testing prevent me from sending our army to your aid."

We nodded in response.

The king motioned toward three men wearing gray cloaks of coarse wool with large hoods that shielded their faces. "We had a difficult time locating scribes who are proficient with weaponry and subterfuge. But after searching the entire realm, we have picked a companion for each of you. Not only will they record the day-to-day occurrences of your Testing as is the custom, but they will step in to protect you if the need arises."

"Your Majesty," I said. "If I face danger and my companion rescues me, then of what benefit is the Testing?"

Sir Axel shared a look with the king as though they'd anticipated such a question.

Though I meant no disrespect, I had to speak up. "I beg your forgiveness, Your Majesty, Sir Axel. I cannot in good conscience accept the aid of my scribe—"

"Nor can I," Kresten and Mikkel said at the same time.

Sir Axel stiffened as if preparing for battle. "They have been instructed not to step in to provide assistance unless you specifically ask for it or are at risk of losing your life."

"Even then," I protested, "I could not welcome the help. For surely I would rather perish than be known as a weak prince who couldn't survive on his own."

"Your courage is commendable." The king shifted his thick royal robe of luxurious bearskin to reveal the sword his father had bestowed upon him at his Testing. "And I have faith each of you shall prevail. Nevertheless, we are ensuring your safety as best we can."

As much as I wanted to argue with the king, I clamped my mouth closed and bowed my head. A moment later, Sir Axel began our introductions to our scribes. And when my companion stepped forward and lowered his hood, I breathed easier. The man was diminutive, thin, and foreign. I couldn't discern his nationality, but from his olive skin, dark hair, and narrowed eyes, I suspected he hailed from one of the exotic nations in the East.

Such a small man could hardly be expected to be my bodyguard. And as a foreigner, would he know the language enough to write down my every action and word during the Testing?

He bowed low. "Your Highness, it will be my pleasure to serve you."

At the smoothness of his greeting without a trace of a foreign accent, I startled. "Thank you . . ."

"My name is Tymur." He switched seamlessly from Scanian to the language of the Great Isle. "But please, call me Ty." Once again his inflection was flawless, perhaps even more so than my own, although my mother had spoken the native tongue of her people so often it was second nature.

"Very well, Ty," I replied in the language of my mother's people. It was as good a time as any to switch, since that's all I would speak in the months ahead. "I hope you are a fast writer, for I shall give you much to record."

Ty stared blankly at me, clearly not much for jesting. And I suspected in the dangerous days to come, I would have to do more rescuing of my new companion than he would of me.

As I faced the west and let the cold wind buffet my cheeks, I braced my shoulders for the trials that would erelong be upon me and prayed someday I would be found worthy.

Chapter 2

Gabriella

"Run faster!" I shouted breathlessly. The sharp claws of rats scraped against the stone, and their bone-chilling squeaks echoed in the narrow cavern, drawing nearer.

Ahead, Benedict's and Alice's footsteps thudded as hard as their old legs could possibly take them. But the past months of exhausting labor had exacted their toll on my faithful servants, and they couldn't move through the winding tunnels with the same agility they'd had after first arriving in the mine pits.

The steep uphill passageway made our race more difficult, as did the gravel that gave way beneath our feet, causing us to slip with nearly every step.

"Make haste!" I urged again, even as a rat lunged toward me and snapped at my leather boot. I slammed my hammer down on its head, causing it to yelp a high-pitched protest as it tumbled back several paces.

The faint light streaming in from the top of the incline meant we weren't far from the safety of the surface. We needed to persevere until we reached the light, where we would escape the danger.

I had only to picture Molly's swollen arm from earlier in the week, the skin purplish-blue and stretched taut, to know the consequence of even the smallest rat bite. I had only to picture the blood and severed limbs from the amputations I'd witnessed. I had only to picture those who survived and returned to the mines, attempting to meet their daily quotas with only one hand or one leg remaining.

Alice stumbled and slid down, nearly bumping into me. With wild eyes, she clutched her chest, her breathing so labored she couldn't speak. Her gray hair had come loose from a simple linen head scarf and was now plastered to her perspiring forehead and cheeks.

"I beseech you, my lady," Benedict said through his own jagged breaths. "Take Alice and I'll fight the fiends."

I swung my hammer at another rat, and he did the same. Could Benedict prevail against the vicious rodents by himself while I helped Alice the rest of the way?

No. With so many, he'd surely be bitten. "We shall slay them together. 'Tis the only way, Benedict."

While fighting, he continued to push upward, practically carrying Alice. His silence meant he opposed my assistance. I couldn't blame him. I wasn't the least bit skilled in wielding weaponry and would likely hinder rather than aid him.

But what choice did we have?

"I am growing more proficient with my hammer and chisel." I ignored the bandages around my fingers, especially the bloodiest one. "You need not worry about me."

A shadow momentarily fell over the opening ahead, and I took sudden hope from it. "Help! Please, help!"

An instant later, a form dropped into the passageway. "Gabi? That be ye?"

"Yes!" I squinted to see the tall, lithe outline of Curly, one of the many kind people who'd befriended me. "The rats are after us!"

Before the words were out of my mouth, Curly was sliding down the gravel. Like Benedict and Alice, I flattened myself against the tunnel wall to make room for him. At the same time I kicked at a rat, sending it rolling away only to have another latch on to my boot and scurry up the leather.

I batted it with my hammer. But this time I missed, and the rodent climbed higher, clutching my frayed skirt, rending the thin linen with its claws and two protruding front teeth.

I couldn't hold back a cry of alarm, and Benedict came to my rescue, slamming the rat away. It fell, taking a section of my skirt with it. In the same moment, he booted and swung and fought the others that leapt at us, ravenous for human blood.

With a shout, Curly plowed into the creatures, his sharpened rock blade already flying and sending the skinny creatures tumbling down the incline. Seconds later, dead or injured rats littered the path, and the cavern grew silent except for our labored breathing.

Curly stared down the darkened passageway, his tall body hunched and his makeshift knife out-stretched, as though he expected more rats to rush at us. "Go on up with ye now." He didn't take his attention from the path. "I'll see to yer backs, that I will."

"Oh, thank you, Curly. You are a godsend."

"Yer the godsend."

I wanted to say more, to thank him again, but at Benedict's tug I resumed the climb upward. Only after we'd crawled through the square opening and onto the rocky mountaintop, did I realize how badly I was shaking. My knees were too weak to hold my weight, and my hands trembled too much to tuck my tools back into my rope belt.

Even so, heedless of the stones that dug into my hands and knees, I crawled over to Benedict and Alice where they'd collapsed, searching them for any signs of blood. "You were not bitten, were you?"

"No," Benedict whispered, grasping Alice's hand. "Thank the saints."

Heads bent in weariness, their stooped shoulders heaved as they gasped in air. Their garments, which had once fit so snugly against plump frames, now hung over sharply protruding bones. Their faces were sallow and sunken, their skin pale, and their bodies bruised.

Empathy swelled inside, and I gathered them both in my arms, kissing the tops of their heads. I loathed that every day I had to watch them waste away a little more.

All around us in the growing dusk, Slave Town was a hustle of business. Smoke drifted from thatched huts, and the scents of the evening meal wafted in the cool air, making my stomach grumble in protest.

I sighed. We would be going without food again tonight, now that we'd left our baskets behind in the mine.

Curly's footsteps crunched in the rocks beside me. "Haven't I told ye to be guarding your flame with your life?"

I released the older couple and turned to find my friend glaring down at me. He was framed by the fading sunlight and the splashes of rose and orange against the mountain peaks to the west. The colors of the setting sun highlighted the red in his wildly curly hair, which was much brighter than my own softer blond-red. His temperament oft flamed like his hair.

"'Twas not our fault." I spoke calmly, trying to keep him from exploding. "We were guarding the flame carefully, but a foul breeze snuffed it out in an instant, plunging us into darkness."

His thick red brows furrowed together above a face that had likely been handsome at one time but was now thin and bony and pale. "If ye won't be working with the rest of us, then ye need to avoid the old tunnels and stay closer to the new where the air is cleaner."

He knew Alice wasn't capable of climbing down to labor in the new drift with the rest of the slaves. We'd already tried on several occasions. And he also knew that being together didn't mean anyone was safe. With the tremors and cave-in that had trapped Molly and two others last week, he should know that well enough. We'd had to work day and night to dig them out, and even then only Molly survived.

"If ye stay closer and then yer light goes, ye can call me, and I'll be there in the twitch of a lamb's tail, that I will."

The rats couldn't abide light, and it was our only protection against their bloodthirstiness. If only Molly's torch had lasted until we'd been able to dig her out of the rubble. At the sudden shadow on Curly's face, I guessed he was thinking the same.

"How is Molly tonight?" I asked.

"She be sitting up and smiling." His haunted eyes darkened as he glanced at the hut used as the infirmary. "So I can't be complaining now, can I?"

Like most of the other slaves, Molly hadn't deserved to be sent to the mines. She and her brother had been present when a group of peasants had rioted over new taxes. They'd been in the wrong place at the wrong time and were rounded up with the dissidents and sent to the mines. I'd just arrived when her brother died of an infection. Still in the midst of grieving, Molly had taken me under her wing and taught me everything I needed to know to survive.

Curly held out a hand to assist me to my feet. "I take it ye left yer buckets behind, then?"

"We had no choice."

"I'd be giving ye some of my rations, but I already divided it up."

No doubt he'd given some of his supper to Molly, and only rightly so. "We shall be fine. Do not trouble yourself over us."

We'd travailed all day, chiseling rock to fill our buckets, rock that was necessary to get our daily ration for meals. 'Twould be of no consequence now. The hatch would soon be battened down for the night to keep any rats from coming to the surface during the darkness. Anyone who remained in the mine would be trapped there for the night, and I couldn't risk that.

A commotion at the bridge drew my attention. Someone was crossing the braided rope structure that stretched across a deep ravine separating the mine from civilization. The suspension bridge was the only way in and out, except most of the people who came to work in the mine as slaves never made it out.

I would be the exception. I didn't know exactly how I would accomplish such a feat. All I knew was that I had to escape before Midsummer's Eve, less than two months away.

"Jolly," Curly muttered as he watched the bridge. "Just what we be needing. A fresh batch of slaves."

New slaves meant more competition for finding the coveted gems that could be used to buy any number of luxuries from clothing to medicine to soap. The emeralds, rubies, sapphires, and diamonds were nearly impossible to locate now. After the past six months of living at the mine, I'd witnessed the discoveries diminishing from several veins a day to several a week. And now we were fortunate to find several in a month.

Most people believed that somehow the sun's midsummer zenith helped the gems to grow and surface every year. Very few were aware of what really caused the precious jewels to reappear after Midsummer's Eve. My father had been one of those few, and it cost him his life.

I was also one of those privy to the truth, although it had taken my father's death to fully understand the depths of depravity Queen Margery had sunk to in order to ensure the gem production continued. Ever since learning of her vile practices, I had one burning goal—to end the evil and avenge my father's death.

Still muttering, Curly strode away, gathering around him the gang of loyal slaves who followed and respected him. A good number of them were missing one limb or another to accidents or rat bites. They crossed over barren-land, which separated the village from the bridge. And they positioned themselves near the tower guardhouse that stood on the edge of Slave Town adjacent to the bridge. They would welcome the newcomers just as they always did—with a show of intimidation.

Although I didn't agree with Curly's methods, I couldn't condemn him. Even though the truly dangerous criminals were locked away in the queen's dungeons, desperation and despair oft led people to do things they wouldn't normally consider. And Curly's control prevented anarchy.

The overseers doled out our rations and made certain we followed all the rules. The armed guards ensured that we didn't try to revolt. But neither the overseers nor guards went down into the mines if it could be helped, which made Curly's leadership all the more important.

"Come," I said gently to Alice as I knelt beside her and slid my arm around her waist. "Let's get you home for the night."

Home. The very word brought a painful lump to my throat. While I missed many things about Rockland, more than anything I missed my father. After he'd died, the grand castle with its many outbuildings didn't feel like home anymore. Once the Duchess of Burgundy and her two daughters had arrived to oversee Rockland, I felt like a stranger there.

"Ah, my lady," Alice replied as I lifted her to her feet, her breathing finally even again. "I ought to be helping you, not relying upon you for my daily needs."

"Nonsense. We must lean upon each other. 'Tis the only way to truly survive."

If only I'd never said anything to the duchess about my faithful servants. Instead, I'd beseeched her for their well-being, asked her to show them mercy. Rather than granting my request, she found twisted pleasure in hurting me even further by expelling Benedict and Alice from service and accusing them of stealing from Rockland's coffers alongside me.

I berated myself every day since then for being so foolish, although I suspected my two faithful servants would have come with me anywhere, regardless of my protests. They'd been like grandparents, stepping in whenever my father traveled, bestowing upon me all the love I'd ever needed. And now they were suffering on my account.

"I'll go see if I can find anything for us to eat." Benedict wearily regarded the dozen or so thatched huts that made up our village at the top of Ruby Mountain. Only rotting stumps remained of the pine, hemlock, and firs that had once graced the level area. Now the surface was barren and rocky from all the crushed stone we brought topside every day in an effort to meet our daily quota of digging.

"Thank you, Benedict." I suspected he'd come home empty-handed as he had the last time. Even if one of the other slaves had an extra piece of fish or bread they were willing to sell, we had naught to exchange in payment. We'd long since used up the few commodities of value we'd been allowed to bring into slavery, and we owned nothing anymore.

From the frustration etched into Benedict's once-distinguished face, he realized the futility of his search as well. And yet, he cared too much about Alice and me not to try to find something for our meal. Perhaps he would pledge his own rations away as he'd done last time.

Alice hobbled next to me as I led her away from the mine entrance. Once I settled her in the hut we shared with several other slaves, I made my way through the growing darkness toward the infirmary. Without any medicine or pain relief, the best I could do for the sick was offer them water and what little food was available. Most of the time, I simply sat at their sides, held their hands, and sang to them. It wasn't much, but kindness was oft the best remedy for an ailment.

Shouting from the overseers at the edge of town drew my attention. A man dangled from a broken slat in the bridge. More than half of the wooden step had vanished, having dropped into the ravine hundreds of feet below. And now the unfortunate newcomer was about to follow suit.

"No," I whispered as my father's voice echoed in my head: *"If someone is in need, 'tis better to try to help, even if you fail, than never to try at all."*

I couldn't just stand by and watch someone fall and die.

Frantically, I glanced around for something—anything—I could use to rescue him. But our town had naught to boast of except hardship and barrenness.

I stumbled forward regardless, tripping over the rocks and nearly falling in my haste to reach the bridge. All the while, I untied the rope around my waist that served as a belt for my mining tools. It wasn't long, but it was something.

One of the newcomers, a thickly muscled man who'd already crossed the ravine, was straining against the hold of the overseers and several other slaves. "Release me! I shall go back for him."

Curly was one of the men attempting to contain the

newcomer. "If ye be stepping on the bridge and getting it moving, yer friend won't be able to hold on."

"He won't be able to hold on as it is!" The man lunged, causing the four or five men at his sides to have to wrestle him back.

Making full use of their distraction, I approached the bridge. As I stepped lightly onto the first slat, I held my breath and hoped the ropes wouldn't sway too much. I was lithe and lightweight, especially after toiling in the mine pits for the past months. If anyone could cross without swaying the bridge, I was the most likely to do so.

I tiptoed several slats in before Curly's anxious command beckoned to me. "Gabi, ye get back here right now, d'ye hear me?"

"You know I am the best choice to make such a rescue," I called over my shoulder.

"No one can be helping him but himself! Now get on back here."

I took another delicate step, praying fervently I wouldn't cause the man to lose his grip. His knuckles were white, but he seemed to have a strong hold, one hand on the broken slat and the other on the cord that ran the length of the bridge. If only I could toss my rope out to him so he had something sturdier to cling to.

As I continued my tentative walk, my thoughts strayed to the day I'd arrived last autumn, to how frightened I'd been to cross the bridge. With each step I'd taken, I hadn't been able to block out the terrible rocky gorge that lay far below. Not only had I feared I'd slip and fall to my death, but I feared crossing to the other side would lead me to the bowels of death itself, to a future so different from anything I'd known that I couldn't fathom how I'd survive.

Of course, my new life was as hard—perhaps harder—than I'd imagined. Yet even though I'd lost everything, I still had so much to give, especially kindness. *"Kindness is a commodity one can never use up."* I recalled more of my father's advice. *"And kindness is a commodity that will always be in demand."* People around me needed it in abundance every day. Like now . . .

"Hold on," I gently urged the dangling man. Drawing closer, I could see he wasn't a man after all, but a lad of twelve or fourteen. What had he done to earn a place in the mine pits? Likely not much. Very few in Slave Town were true criminals. Most were simply victims in a land where justice rarely prevailed and mercy was nonexistent.

Only six slats away now, I met the young man's gaze. His pupils were dark and wild with fear.

"I shall throw you this rope, and I want you to use it along with the side of the bridge to heft yourself back up." And while he did so, I'd pray for the strength to hoist him. "Do you think you can do that?"

He nodded, even as his fingers against the slat began to slip. He hastened to readjust his hold, the veins in his wrists and fingers protruding from his effort at hanging on.

"Gabi, get back here!" Curly's shout was loaded with urgency. "Why can't ye be thinking about yerself for once?"

I ignored my friend. He gave me too much credit and praised me too oft for taking care of others. What he didn't see was the bitterness eating away at me since my father's death—an ugly part of me, festering and growing and at times choking off my singing.

After two more steps, I was close enough. I looped and knotted the rope around my arm and then tossed the rest of the length toward the lad. It fell close to his hand but not close enough. I dragged it back and threw it again, this time hitting his knuckles.

"Ready?" I grabbed on to the bridge's handhold to brace myself.

"Ready." He heaved a breath, then let go of the slat and lunged for the rope. He fumbled for a moment, dangling by one arm from the side of the bridge. I was vaguely aware of shouting and tussling behind me, but I had to focus if I had any chance of saving this young man.

I leaned in and shoved the rope so it draped over the edge of the slat where, hopefully, he could see it. He groped frantically and managed to wrap his fingers around it. The moment he had a hold, his weight nearly yanked me off my slat. But I held fast, even as the knot tied to my arm sawed into my skin, twisting the tender flesh.

"Come now," I said with as much encouragement as I could. "You can do this."

The commotion behind me grew louder, and I thought I heard Benedict's voice raised in alarm. No doubt he was attempting to come after me, and someone was detaining him. I could only pray they would succeed and he'd remain safely on level ground. If anything happened to him, Alice wouldn't be able to survive.

The young man pulled on the rope again, and this time managed to drag himself up until he was clinging to the next slat. As he gripped the wood with both hands and lifted his body onto it, the pressure against my wrist subsided, and I released the tension in my shoulders.

We'd done it. He was safe.

"Careful!" came a shout from the end of the bridge.

In the next second, the sound of splintering wood filled the air. The board beneath the youth ripped into two pieces. Panic once again flashed across his face as he hung on to the sliver that remained.

I held myself motionless, willing him to press onward.

But the rotting wood crumbled beneath his fingers, and he began to fall, dragging me with him.

Chapter 3

VILMAR

I WRENCHED LOOSE FROM MY CAPTORS AND DARTED TOWARD THE bridge. Though several of the men leapt after me, I was too quick now that I was free.

If they'd allowed me to go back for Farthing as I requested, then the young woman wouldn't have gone onto the bridge. And now instead of losing one person, we were at risk of losing two.

As I flew across the slats, the bridge rocked from side to side. But the movement was of no concern this time. Only speed mattered.

Somehow she managed to grab the edge of the bridge, whereupon she released a desperate cry, as though trying to summon inner fortitude. Nevertheless, the weight of the boy pulling on her arm was too much. Her bandaged and bloodied fingers were slipping.

With mere seconds before Farthing dragged them both down to their deaths, I threw myself the last distance and caught her arm.

"Grab on to me!" I commanded, digging into her flesh

and stopping her descent.

She grasped me, her fingers tightening around my wrist in return.

I hoisted her high enough for me to clutch the rope binding her to the lad. As I held the weight of both of them, the slats beneath me begin to crack. I needed to get off the bridge with haste. The structure could hardly bear my weight, much less all three of us.

I'd known the bridge was unsafe from the moment I first stepped onto it when making the crossing. In fact, I'd warned the others to tread on the outer edges of the boards and not to put their full weight into the middle. But the lad hadn't heeded my advice.

Behind me, at my waist, I felt a sudden tug. "Pull," Ty said in his usual calm tone.

With Ty's strength added to mine, I scrambled backward, dragging the pair upward and onto the bridge. Thankfully, neither weighed much.

As more slats gave way, I towed the woman back with me. Ty did the same with Farthing. The boards crumbled in rapid succession, but within seconds we made it to solid ground.

Jagged stones covered the mountaintop. Even so, I knelt, bringing the woman down onto my knees. With the weight that had pulled against her arm, her shoulder had been dislocated. Before she could protest, I jerked her joint back into place.

She sucked in a sharp breath, then her eyes fluttered closed, but not before I saw the pain radiating there. As Ty worked to loosen the knot around her wrist, I ran my hand over her arm, checking for broken bones. But other than bloody and chafed skin from rope burn, she hadn't sustained additional injuries.

A ragged-looking man with graying hair pushed his way to my side. "My lady." His voice vibrated with distress. "Oh, my lady."

"She has succumbed to unconsciousness," I said. "But she will be well enough once she awakens."

The men who'd restrained me crowded around us now too, their expressions grave as they regarded the woman. The one with the red hair had been the first to meet me when I'd stepped off the bridge, and his greeting had been a fist in my gut along with a sharp knife pressed into my ribs. The blood he'd drawn was still seeping into my tunic. "I'm in charge here," he'd said in a low tone so the guards couldn't hear him. "Ye do what I say, and we'll get along just fine. D'ye hear me?"

I'd heard him and nodded my acquiescence. I had no wish to make enemies my first day in the mine pits. In fact, my philosophy was not to make enemies on any day of the week. If the red-haired man was some sort of leader amongst the slaves, then I was more than agreeable to following his orders and respecting him, so long as he respected me in return.

Now he stared down at the young woman. The anger he'd been spouting at the woman moments ago disappeared. And in its place fear marked his ashen face. "Is she hurt?"

"She had a great deal of strain upon her shoulders and arm." I lifted her as I stood. "But I don't detect severe injuries."

As I settled her against my chest, I couldn't keep from noticing that she had red hair too. Except hers was a lighter, softer red like the fur of a newborn fawn. Her face, while streaked with dirt, was undeniably beautiful. Long lashes rested against her high-boned cheeks. She had an elegant nose and full, rosy lips.

She was obviously a favorite of the men and for good reason.

"Where shall I take her?" I asked the redhead. "Her arm will need tending and bandaging."

With a nod, he started across a barren strip of land guarded by several soldiers in a tower positioned next to the bridge. With their bows and arrows at the ready, I guessed they wouldn't hesitate to shoot at any man who stepped foot onto the bridge. Perhaps they would have shot me if I'd attempted to rescue Farthing. Maybe this man's efforts at restraining me had been for my protection more than anything.

Now he headed for a cluster of dilapidated thatched huts made of wattle and daub, none of which looked sturdy enough to house livestock much less humans. I followed him, nonetheless, to one of the dwellings. Ducking low, he entered the dark interior.

I hesitated merely a moment before I stepped inside after him. Red coals gleamed in a small center fire pit and gave off enough light for me to see the red-haired man. He knelt next to an old woman lying on a pallet who was covered with a tattered blanket. At his low words, she released a cry of dismay and pushed herself up.

"Lay Lady Gabriella here." She crawled onto the dirt floor and patted the place she'd vacated.

Lady Gabriella? Why was a noblewoman living as a slave in the Gemstone Mountain mine?

As I lowered her to the pallet, she groaned but remained unconscious. The ragged old man now knelt next to the elderly woman. Their once-elegant garments and gentle mannerisms indicated the couple had been servants in Lady Gabriella's household.

Although my curiosity was heightened, I exited the hut to find myself face-to-face with the redheaded man. Night had fallen, and I couldn't make out his expression, but I stiffened in readiness for the rest of my initiation into slavery. What would this man and his minions require of me? Groveling? Extra work? Payment of some kind?

"Thank ye for saving Gabi," he said gruffly.

I was taken aback by his gratitude and struggled to find a response. What relationship did this man have with the young noblewoman? He clearly cared about her. "I could do nothing less—"

He grabbed my tunic and jerked me up, cutting off my words. "Don't ye be getting any ideas about her. Stay far away from her, d'ye hear me?" He twisted my tunic around my neck, choking me.

"I hear you," I managed through my constricted airway.

"If ye touch her again, I won't be thinking twice about cutting off yer hand."

This man must have already claimed Lady Gabriella for himself and wanted to make certain I understood it. The thought of a noblewoman in the clutches of a baseborn man like this made me ill. And yet, what could I do about it? I hadn't come to the mine pits to get involved with the people who languished here. I was here for my Testing, to bear the weight of heavy labor and to persevere under harsh conditions. In so doing, I would prove myself the most worthy to become the next king of Scania.

He choked me for several more seconds, then shoved me back into the hut. I dragged in a gasp of air and watched him stride away with his companions.

If only I could reveal the truth about my identity and purpose in being here. If men like the redheaded leader understood I posed no threat to them and their position, they'd leave me alone to focus on my Testing.

I'd simply have to show them my willingness to cooperate by abstaining from meddling in the affairs of everyone else—particularly abstaining from Lady Gabriella.

My first week working in the mine pits became a blur of exhaustion. I rapidly learned what was expected of the slaves every day—that each man and woman was required to fill a large wooden bucket with chiseled rock as payment for food rations. Failure to produce the daily quota to the overseers in charge of distribution meant hunger.

I also realized soon enough how difficult a task filling one bucket was, much less transporting it to the surface. During my first few days, like the handful of other new slaves, I struggled to chisel a sufficient amount with our dull tools, though I labored nonstop from dawn until dusk.

I was surprised that with all the digging away of the rock we didn't find any gems. Little by little, I came to understand Warwick's Gemstone Mountains were nearly barren of the jewels that had once made the country so wealthy. Those slaves who happened to find the rare stones were the lucky ones allowed to exchange the gems for more food or better clothing or an additional blanket.

By the beginning of my second week, I was able to dig faster, completing my quota well ahead of sundown. Rather than returning to the surface once my container was full, as some of the other seasoned workers did, I stayed and assisted Ty and the new slaves.

While we worked in the main tunnel near everyone, we remained outsiders, not yet having earned the trust and acceptance I hoped would come with time. I learned the redheaded leader was called Curly, and even though he was abrasive and quick-tempered, he seemed to have the best interests of the slaves at heart, solving disputes and keeping order.

I also learned none of the slaves condemned to the mines were hardened criminals. They were mostly ordinary citizens who'd been charged with insignificant offenses that were undeserving of hard labor as punishment. Had Queen Margery purposely tasked her officials with rounding up people on a regular basis in order to maintain the mines?

"Heard tell some of the rats be big as full-growed dogs." Farthing leaned against the granite wall where he'd made little progress that day. The lad had recovered from the near-death experience on the bridge and had easily adjusted to life in the mine.

As I hammered the handle of my chisel and broke off another chunk of stone, my gaze touched on the closest torch, the long end wedged into a crack in the wall. Several more torches belonging to other slaves burned at intervals along the drift to keep rats at bay.

"Guess they have to be big if they're a-tearing off arms and legs," Farthing continued.

"The rats aren't tearing them off," responded Ernie, a portly, middle-aged man who'd worked as a cook in the royal palace in Kensington until he'd been accused of poisoning the food of one of the queen's personal priests. "Apparently, they're only biting. But the bite causes some kind of disease that can only be stopped by amputation."

"Amputation?" Farthing tossed several rocks into the air in an attempt at juggling. He was more content to watch the work than participate, an attitude which likely contributed to his propensity to pick pockets for the farthings after which he'd been nicknamed. "What's an amputation?"

"Cutting off the diseased limb." Ernie mopped his perspiring brow and fanned his overheated face.

I'd expected the mine pits to be cold, and the temperature did decrease during the initial descent of a hundred or more feet. But at some point, the air grew warm again, making us too hot as we worked so that some of the slaves shed layers of clothing.

Farthing paused his juggling and seemed to contemplate the problem of lost limbs. He glanced in the direction of the nearest group of slaves. Of the six or so, two were missing body parts—one, a hand, and the second, half his leg. I admired their tenacity to prevail in the harsh conditions rather than giving up in despair.

"Maybe it's not the rats," Farthing continued. "What if it be the wraiths a-biting people?"

Ernie nodded and then launched into one of his stories about the wraiths deep in the mountains rousing as the tunnels drew closer to their resting spots.

At the sight of Curly climbing nimbly up a rock wall using the simple hand and foot holds that had been notched out of stone, I let my tools fall idle. He must be going once more to check on Lady Gabriella, who worked up a level with her servants, whose names I'd learned were Benedict and Alice.

I'd expected to see Lady Gabriella with the others down in the mine. But I'd learned her old maidservant couldn't navigate the narrow shaft that led to the newest drift, so Lady Gabriella stayed with the couple. Curly had grumbled about the danger of the three working alone, but he made no effort to force them to labor with everyone else, though he'd threatened to do so.

I'd done as Curly instructed and kept my distance from Lady Gabriella. In fact, the morning after the accident, when she'd sought me at our hut, Ty had accepted her thanks, while I'd remained out of sight until she went on her way.

In spite of my resolve to stay far away from her, my curiosity grew, and I found I couldn't ignore her—not when everyone adored her, including the overseers and guards. It was easy to see why, when she spent most of her evenings in the infirmary with the sick and maimed. When her sweet songs filtered through the town. When she offered words of encouragement everywhere she went.

Of course, it didn't help that Farthing practically worshipped her for rescuing him and rambled on about her at least a dozen times a day. The lad claimed she was a saint. After watching her walk out onto the bridge to save Farthing without a moment of hesitation, I was easily persuaded to agree with the assessment.

Ernie finished his story and uncorked his leather drinking pouch. "Some even say the wraiths have the power to make the gems grow in the rocks every year."

Farthing's eyes widened. "So, if we find a wraith, we might find real gems?"

In the process of tilting the pouch to his lips, Ernie paused and glanced around before he lowered his voice. "Only after the priests come down into the mines and sprinkle the holy water. Then the wraiths start making the gems again."

With a shake of my head, I returned my attention to the granite and tapped my hammer to the chisel. "Best get to working, Farthing," I said with as much sternness as I could muster. "Or at dusk we may have to leave you to the rats and wraiths with your empty bucket."

I could feel Ty watching me with his keen gaze, and as usual I sensed his judgment. Each night by the glow of the coals, he recorded the day's events, including my every word and action no matter how insignificant. The rules of the Testing prohibited me from reading his journal or attempting to influence what he wrote there. Thus, I guarded my words and behavior carefully, wanting him to see and record only the very best so that when the king and the Lagting read his report, they'd be impressed by how I handled myself.

A faint scream echoed from the direction of the shaft where Curly had disappeared.

I paused and listened but then forced myself to keep tapping. Although Farthing claimed Curly had a woman, I still couldn't shake the intuition that the redheaded leader was interested in more from Lady Gabriella than mere friendship.

At another scream, this one more distinct, the clanking of hammers and chisels died away to silence. All eyes turned toward the shaft, and faces grew taut with fear.

Though my rational side told me I needed to remain safe and away from any conflict, I couldn't keep from thinking about Lady Gabriella's courage the day she'd saved Farthing. If any plight had befallen her whatsoever, she deserved to have someone come to her aid.

As the pressure inside built, I tucked my hammer and chisel into my rope belt. What harm could come from checking on the lady? Surely a furtive peek wouldn't cause any conflict with Curly.

Without another moment of hesitation, I headed to the shaft and began the climb.

"Take a torch." Ty held out the flaming stick.

With a nod, I took it from him and continued my ascent. He would follow erelong since he took his role as my bodyguard as seriously as he did his scribe duties.

As I crawled up into the next level, I lifted the torch and listened carefully. At the distant sounds of scratching and squeaking from a tunnel to the west, my muscles stiffened. Though I'd yet to see one of the deadly rats, I wasn't about to underestimate them. I unsheathed my seax from the sheath-like compartment in the sole of my boot and took off at a run.

The low, jagged ceiling and winding path slowed my pace. But as the noises grew louder, I pushed myself faster.

"They're gaining on us!" Curly shouted.

Upon rounding a bend, I halted at the sight of the horde of rats scurrying just inches behind Curly, Lady Gabriella, and her two old servants. Curly was doing his best to fend them off whenever one latched on to him or Lady Gabriella, but the older couple wasn't able to go fast enough to outrace the rodents.

I raised my torch higher, hoping to shine it upon the rats to slow them down since apparently the light hurt their eyes. But the flames seemed to have the opposite effect, making them scuttle faster to outrun the light.

If the brightness was hurting them, there was only one thing left to do.

"Curly! Catch!" Whether he was ready or not, I tossed the torch. It soared through the air and clattered to the ground behind him, knocking into several rats. The flames touched their brittle hair and ignited them.

At the growing flames and heat, the remaining creatures stopped and screeched. The brilliance temporarily blinded them. To escape the glow, they turned, squeaking in both terror and anger, and they scampered toward me.

I crouched and prepared for battle.

Chapter 4

Gabriella

I was frozen in place. I needed to continue onward, helping Benedict and Alice reach the safety of the surface, but I couldn't move. I could only stare down the passageway at the new slave who'd somehow appeared from nowhere and was now preparing to single-handedly combat a pack of rats.

At the very least, I ought to rush to his aid. Or encourage Curly to help him. But my friend was standing and staring with as much shock as I was as the new slave swung his hammer at one rat and slashed at another with what appeared to be a knife.

I'd heard some of the others referring to him as Vilmar, and all week I'd been curious about the man who'd risked his life for me. But when I'd gone to his hut to thank him, his olive-skinned companion came to the door and informed me Vilmar was indisposed.

Taken aback by the rude refusal to see me, I'd done my best to put Vilmar out of my mind. The task was made more difficult because the other slaves oft talked of him, admiring his strength and good looks as well as his humility. Even Curly had a measure of regard for Vilmar he normally didn't hold for new slaves.

Now as the scorched flesh of the burning rats rose into the air along with the shrieking of the others, Vilmar expertly wielded his knife, slitting throats and slicing open one rat after another, until within seconds they lay dead at his feet.

When finished, he toed the heap, his weapons poised to finish off any rodent that moved. The curved blade was coated in blood and should have repelled me, but I couldn't stop staring at it.

Such weapons were forbidden, and the overseers would flog Vilmar if they caught him with it. And though the overseers allowed our mining tools, we had to subject them to periodic checks to make sure they remained dull. Some, like Curly, sharpened stones to use as weapons. But being caught with a sharp rock was cause for flogging as well.

Ever since I'd started formulating my plan for revenge, I knew I needed a weapon to kill Grendel. Once I had a weapon, I needed someone to train me to use it. Although I'd been sharpening a stone to use, my efforts were feeble. And I was running out of time.

With the attention on his knife, Vilmar lowered it. I caught the movement of his olive-skinned companion behind him, close enough to help yet a safe distance away.

Curly bent and retrieved the torch without taking his gaze from Vilmar.

"I heard screaming," Vilmar said, as though explaining his presence to Curly. "I hope no one is hurt." He peered beyond us to where Benedict and

Alice stood, their shoulders hunched and faces shadowed.

"Our light went out again." I squeezed first Benedict's, then Alice's hands, reassuring myself they were unharmed. "And it only takes a few minutes of darkness for the rats to come out."

"Then none of you were bitten?"

I started to shake my head, but Curly spoke first. "It be too close this time, Gabi. Too close. What if I'd waited to check on ye for another five minutes?"

"We would have outrun them." I infused my voice with confidence, but I wasn't so sure that we could have. I had only to think of last week when we'd started up the steepest passageway and how slow Alice had been. If not for Curly's rescue, we surely would have been bitten.

Curly held the torch over the remains of the charred rats. Vilmar had acted decisively by throwing the flaming stick. Not only had he killed some with the fire, but he'd diverted the rest away from us straight into the blade of his knife.

"Ye need to be staying with the group from now on," Curly said, as he had after the last rat escapade.

"You know I cannot."

"I'll not be giving ye a choice this time." Curly jutted his chin, the torchlight highlighting the jagged scars along his jaw, his cheeks, and even on his forehead.

I set my shoulders and would have pulled myself up to my full height of five feet, four inches, but I'd learned during the early days of slavery not to bump the sharp rocks that formed the ceiling. "I refuse to leave Alice and Benedict to fend for themselves."

"You must go." Benedict spoke forcefully, as he always did whenever I got into this argument with Curly. "All we want is for you to be safe."

"And all I want is for *you* to be safe."

"Your two servants can come with," Vilmar cut in.

"'Tis not possible." I attempted to keep the exasperation from my tone. After all, Vilmar wouldn't know the details of the situation, how Alice had nearly slipped and fallen to her death the last time we'd gone with the others. "The climb up and down the shaft is too treacherous."

"If we combine our rope belts, we can fashion a sling to lower and raise them through the shaft."

A sling? Why hadn't we considered that before?

"We could also use such a lift to hoist the full buckets at the end of the workday." Vilmar watched Curly expectantly. "That is, if Curly is agreeable."

Curly was silent, his expression guarded. "It might work."

"We can try, can we not?" This time Vilmar looked directly at me. His eyes were a light crystal-blue that seemed to see right through me to the deepest secrets of my heart. I realized in that moment the rumors regarding his good looks were entirely true. Not only were his eyes a beautiful color, but everything about him was beautiful—his chiseled face, muscular frame, and even his broad hands. His jaw and chin had a layer of scruff, and his brown hair was overlong and pulled back into a leather strip. Nevertheless, he held himself with the bearing of nobility and not a common man.

Who was he? And how had he ended up as a slave in the mine pits? Of course rumors were already circulating that he'd displeased his father and, as punishment, was sent here. But I sensed this man's story ran deeper than he'd revealed.

We retrieved our buckets and made our way to the shaft that led to the newest drift. Curly made quick work of descending and gathering up as many ropes as we needed to assemble the sling. Vilmar tied the knots and then lowered Alice down without so much as a scratch. By the time we were all back at work, I doubled my efforts at chipping away the rock. Because of the lost time, we would be hard-pressed to meet our daily quota. Thus, I was surprised when I dumped a handful of crumbling stone into Alice's bucket, that it was nearly full.

"Vilmar insisted I take his." Alice darted a look at the handsome slave pounding his chisel into stone. He'd rolled up his sleeves, revealing muscles bulging with each forceful blow.

I couldn't tear my sights away from his rippling arms. "That was generous of him."

"He gave some of his rocks to Benedict too."

"When?"

"When you were distracted in talking with Farthing."

As though sensing my attention, Vilmar looked up and caught my gaze. In that instant, as earlier, I could feel his keen assessment, that he was trying to analyze me every bit as much as I was him.

He slid a glance in Curly's direction at the forefront of the drift before focusing once again on his chisel. Curly had obviously warned Vilmar against interacting with me, which explained the rebuff earlier in the week when I'd attempted to thank him.

At times Curly's concern was overbearing.

However, I couldn't complain, not when my friend had made sure I was safe from the wiles of any men who might find me attractive.

While I didn't want to put Vilmar into danger from Curly, I needed to speak with him privately. Soon.

Even in late spring, the predawn air on the top of Ruby Mountain always dipped below freezing. As I waited in the shadows of the infirmary, I tried to quell my shivering, clutching my threadbare cloak around me tighter and forcing away thoughts of the thick white coat trimmed in rabbit fur I'd worn in winters past along with the leather boots lined with warm flannel. I'd had more muffs and hats than I'd known what to do with.

What I wouldn't give to have just one of each now.

I released a soft sigh that puffed out as a frozen white cloud in the frigid air. As the daughter of the richest nobleman in Warwick, I'd taken so much of my privileged life for granted, and I regretted now that I hadn't been more appreciative of all I once owned. It wasn't that I'd been ungrateful. I'd simply been oblivious to how comfortable and easy my life was . . . until it had been ripped away from me.

At a slight movement near one of the men's huts, I held myself motionless, forcing my shivering to abate. Was it Vilmar? Would he meet with me as I'd requested?

Through the sliver of moonlight, I strained to see whether anyone was coming my way. But the town was eerily still, the overseers slumbering and the night guards finishing their watch.

At the crunch of gravel behind me, I spun. A cloaked man stood close enough that he could have grabbed and muffled me if he'd been so inclined. But from the way he held himself slightly aloof, I guessed this was Vilmar even before he lowered his hood.

"My lady," he whispered, leaving me no doubt he'd guessed my nobility. 'Twas no secret anyway. Soon after I'd arrived at the mine pits, everyone had learned the story about my fall from the duchess's favor.

"My lord." I let him know he couldn't hide his nobility from me any more than I could mine from him.

I thought I detected his lips quirking up into the semblance of a smile, even as he peered past the shadows of my hood as though curious to discern more about my reason for requesting the meeting.

I pushed the hood away, letting it drop to my back and giving him full view of my countenance—or at least as much of it as was possible to see in the darkness.

I was still struck by the beauty of his eyes, so intense and yet tender. They were the kind of eyes that spoke of both pain and joy, of tribulation and laughter, of past sorrows yet promises for tomorrow.

At this close range, his strength and his power were more imposing. And yet, somehow I sensed I was as safe with him as I was with Curly.

Though he was nobility, I'd never met him in any of the social circles I was a part of when my father was alive. Of course, I'd still been too young at that time to participate fully in court life, and I'd been content to remain at home.

After Father died and the Duchess of Burgundy took over managing Rockland, I'd attended a few social events until I garnered more attention than her daughters and the duchess insisted on my absence. Even at those rare opportunities, I'd never seen him. Of that I was certain. He had a face a person would never forget.

"So, my lady." His gaze roamed languidly, making me suddenly forget about the cold. "Ty said your request was urgent."

As I'd climbed to the surface yesterday with our heavy loads of rocks, I managed to fall into step next to Ty during one wider stretch. I whispered to him that I needed to meet with Vilmar outside the infirmary right before the break of day. But now, for the life of me, I couldn't remember the request.

"Well?" His voice hinted at a smile. From his tone and the ease with which he spoke, he was clearly practiced around women.

I scrambled to come up with something. "I have not had the opportunity to thank you yet."

"Yes, that is very urgent. I can see why you needed to meet so secretly for it."

"It is urgent. Especially since you have chosen to ignore me at every turn."

"I've chosen to keep my fingers and hands from being severed by your lover."

"Lover?" The word came out on a note of horror.

"Curly."

"Curly is not my lover," I hissed. "He has gallantly taken it upon himself to act as my protector. That is all."

"He fancies himself in love with you."

"He is no more than a friend and brother. He cares about Molly."

"I haven't seen him with any other woman but you."

"Molly is still in the infirmary."

At the rumble of voices nearby, he stiffened.

I sensed we had little time remaining, and I forced my thoughts into a semblance of coherency. "In addition to thanking you for saving me on the bridge as well as rushing to aid us yesterday, I would be grateful if you would instruct me how to . . . kill with a knife."

His lips stalled around his response, and his eyes widened.

"I need to begin training immediately." I swallowed the bile that formed at the thought of taking a life and forced myself to focus on the plan I'd formulated before falling asleep last night. "Today when you see me leave the main drift, you must wait two minutes and then follow."

He shook his head, his jaw tightening.

His protest matched the protest my father would have offered if he'd been alive. In fact, my father's voice rebuked me as it had been for the past hour: *If you give way to violence and hatred, you will only breed bitterness.* But there was no other way to eliminate Grendel. "We shall not have long to train, but every little bit will help—"

"No." His whisper was harsh. "I refuse to train anyone to kill—"

"Would you have me remain defenseless?"

My question gave him pause. As I'd anticipated, he was an empathetic man who could be moved by plight and pity. Although I had no intention of sharing my true plans, I needed to reveal enough to convince him. "I must learn how to slay my enemy, or I myself shall most certainly perish."

"What enemy?"

"I cannot speak the name. Nonetheless, 'tis an enemy I must face in less than two months' time, and if I do not know how to kill him, I shall die at his hands."

"I don't understand." His forehead wrinkled. "I have been in the mine but a fortnight, and already 'tis evident everyone here loves you. No one would dare harm a hair on your head, much less kill you."

"I have not spoken of this enemy to anyone else. But when I saw your knife yesterday, I knew you were the one who could help train me."

He glanced around again. "Then you are at risk even now?"

"No. I have two months."

His attention came to rest upon me, and he studied my face as though seeking answers there. I couldn't share the truth of my plans, lest anyone attempt to stop me.

"If someone sees you with the knife, you could be flogged." He threw out what seemed to be a last weak protest.

"Likewise, for you."

"I am willing to take the risk."

"So am I."

He pursed his lips.

"Please." I infused my voice with as much pleading as I could muster. "You are my only hope."

Seconds ticked by, and the town began to awaken around us—the clank of a cooking pot, ragged coughing, and low murmuring voices.

Finally, Vilmar released a short, tense breath. "The only way we can spend time together without rousing suspicion is if we pretend to be"—he paused as though searching for the right words—"*enamored* with each other."

A strange flush rose into my cheeks. I knew exactly what he was referring to. Down in the mine pits, couples who wanted time alone would sneak off for short periods. Of course, they never wandered beyond the glimmer of torchlight and never stayed away for long. But no one questioned the need for the couple to have a few moments to themselves once in a while.

Even so, I hesitated at using such a ruse. It was one thing to sneak away undetected. It was another thing entirely to flaunt our leaving and allow people to believe we were courting.

In the world I'd come from, noble young ladies did not court without the benefit of a chaperone. I had no doubt Alice or Benedict would insist on accompanying me, and then they would know of my training and ask me all sorts of unwanted questions.

"I cannot lie to Alice or Benedict."

"Then you shall have to work hastily at becoming enamored with me to prevent a lie."

"One cannot force oneself to become enamored."

His smile broke free. "No woman has ever had to force herself to like me."

I could only imagine how true his statement was. He was not only good-looking, but he exuded a blatantly masculine aura that had drawn me in during our brief interaction, making me like him more, not less.

The truth was, his plan would allow for more training time. In fact, we would have much more freedom to be together if everyone assumed we were a couple.

"I must confess, I shall not find it disagreeable to become enamored with you." His low whisper contained a note of intimacy that made my stomach flutter. "But first, you must inform Curly you are attracted to me and wish to spend time with me."

"You expect me to deceive Curly as well?" My tone rose, and I quickly dropped it to a whisper. "You ask too much, my lord." I straightened my shoulders and lifted my chin, needing to prove both to him and myself I had no attraction whatsoever. I simply admired him for his good and brave deeds. That was all.

He raised a hand as though to caress my cheek, but then apparently thought better of it and crossed his arms over his chest. "My lady, if what you say is true, that you really are in such peril, then allowing yourself to become enamored with me is the least of your problems."

Without waiting for my response, he spun and disappeared as quietly as he came.

I could only stand and watch the early dawn mist swallow him. What harm could come of allowing some innocent attraction to develop between us? As he boasted, he would be an easy man to like. Even if I had to fabricate some of the feelings, surely God would forgive me for my deception, especially because as a result, I would finally be able to put an end to the most dreaded custom in the land.

Chapter 5

VILMAR

CURLY KNELT NEXT TO A YOUNG WOMAN IN THE INFIRMARY AND spoke to her as he smoothed her hair away from her forehead. She must be Molly, the woman Lady Gabriella had mentioned, the one Curly cared about.

By the glow of the hearth, I watched from outside the doorway. I couldn't deny I was more than a little relieved to discover Curly already had a woman and that Lady Gabriella wasn't a pawn in the redheaded leader's hands.

My relief had nothing to do with desiring the beautiful noblewoman for myself. Because I most certainly didn't want her, and I couldn't mislead her in thinking we had a future together or allow myself to become distracted from my Testing. I'd been hesitant to meet with her this morn for that very reason and had almost skipped.

My gaze touched on Lady Gabriella's bent head as she finished bandaging the stump at Molly's elbow. The golden red of her hair never failed to draw my attention, just as it had yesterday after she started working in the drift with the rest of us. She wore it plaited in a single braid that fell to her waist, but that gave full view of her delicate features, her smooth skin, and her graceful figure.

The other slaves claimed the lady had once been lauded as the fairest maiden in the land, and I could see why. Apparently, she'd also been one of the wealthiest, until her father died and Queen Margery pilfered the lands and wealth away from Lady Gabriella.

From the first moment I'd risked my life pulling her and Farthing off the bridge, I sensed she would upend my life. After resisting her since then, I should have continued keeping my distance. But I hadn't been able to stay away from the clandestine meeting, no matter how loudly my internal warning had clanged.

When she'd pleaded with me to teach her how to kill her enemy, the anxiety in her eyes and the desperation etched into her face made it impossible to say no. And I still couldn't, not when I imagined what danger awaited her.

Though she hadn't wanted to reveal her enemy, I guessed she feared her accuser coming to silence her, probably the duchess's steward who had blamed her for stealing. Of course, I'd easily learned about Lady Gabriella's crime. The other slaves spoke freely and had been all too willing to tell me everything I wanted to know about the comely noblewoman.

Now here I was, waiting to begin our charade. But first, I wanted to make sure she followed through in telling Curly about us. Even if I had earned more of his approval after yesterday's rescue, I couldn't jeopardize our tentative peace and risk his wrath.

As Curly started to rise, his attention snagged on me, and he shot a glare my way before he bent to say something in Lady Gabriella's ear. Her head snapped up, and I found myself looking into her expressive blue eyes, which were filled with an anticipation that made my stomach do a strange flip.

I gave her a curt nod, hoping she understood that if she hadn't yet spoken to Curly of our relationship, she needed to do so now. If Curly didn't approve of me for Lady Gabriella, then I wasn't sure what we would do.

With a new rosy hue painting her cheeks, Lady Gabriella said something to the redhead. His brow wrinkled, and the two argued in hushed tones back and forth for at least a full minute.

Several other patients lying on pallets slumbered through the commotion. Finally, Molly raised her uninjured arm and pressed her hand against Curly's face. At the touch, the frustration disappeared and was replaced with a tenderness that made me like Curly better than I did already.

Molly craned her neck to look at me, and I caught a glimpse of her face, thin and pale but kind. She said something more, and it must have been enough, for when Curly rose, he crossed to the door and passed by me without even a glance.

Regardless, I sensed I hadn't heard the last from him. He still didn't trust me, and I had no doubt he'd find a way to threaten me again. In the meantime, it was clear he was attempting to respect both Molly's and Lady Gabriella's wishes.

A moment later, Molly peeked at me again and then whispered something to Lady Gabriella that embarrassed her. Or at least from the way the beautiful noblewoman smiled before ducking her head, I assumed it was something more personal.

Outside, the first pinkish orange of the rising sun tinged the eastern edge of the Gemstone Mountain Range. Low clouds hovered below the tips of the peaks, reminding me of the home I'd left behind over three weeks ago.

Thankfully, the sea voyage to the Great Isle had been uneventful. When the longship had reached a secluded cove along Warwick's central coast, Ty and I had waded ashore and begun our journey by foot to the mountain range at the heart of the country. We'd avoided roads and rivers, opting instead for secluded trails until we'd reached our contact, Lord Kennard, a longtime friend of my father's who'd once been an ambassador to Scania. He'd then made arrangements for his guards to escort us the rest of the distance to the mine.

Since arriving, I'd been too concerned with surviving to pay much attention to the surroundings or to think about home. But now, with the beauty of the dawn sky, I felt at peace with my Testing. I'd survived the beginning difficult days, the uncertainty of the work, the danger of everything that lurked in the depths of the mountains. I'd made friends with the other new slaves. And I hadn't made an enemy of the leader—or at least I prayed Curly wouldn't slit my throat tonight in my sleep. Things were going better than I could have predicted.

"You need not wait for me," Lady Gabriella murmured as she exited the infirmary.

I guessed she would have ignored me as Curly had, except Molly was watching. Instead, she paused, allowing me enough time to offer half the roll I'd saved from breaking my fast.

She glanced away from the roll, but not before I caught sight of the hunger in her eyes. She had fed the last of her rations to Molly, leaving none for herself. It wasn't the first time I'd noticed her giving her food to others. Whenever anyone failed to make their quota, Lady Gabriella was always the first to share with those in need, eating something only at Benedict's insistence.

Of course, I could do nothing to change the system of exchange that kept the slaves digging and thus too exhausted and weak to revolt. I hadn't come to the mine pits to try to right the wrongs or eradicate slavery. All I could do was ensure I was learning to serve others and live out my challenge to be the slave of all.

"Take it, my lady." I thrust the roll into her hand.

With Molly's gaze still upon us, Lady Gabriella was left with no choice but to accept it.

"You could try smiling at me," I whispered. "A smile might convince our audience that you like me more than the glare will."

Forthwith, her lips lifted into a smile, one that nearly rendered me speechless with its beauty. Had I yet seen her smile? Surely, I would have remembered it if she had. For someone who brought so much joy to others, she deserved to be happy every day and all throughout each day. What could I do to give her more to smile about?

From the sad slant of her eyes, she obviously hadn't had much happiness here or before she'd arrived. What had her life been like?

As we made our way to the hatch, she nibbled on her roll. "You need not spend every moment with me," she said when we were out of earshot of others.

"We must put forth some effort at being seen as a couple." I leaned closer so our arms brushed. "Or people may suspect other motives for our being together."

She chewed and seemed to contemplate my words.

"What do you suggest we do to convince everyone?"

At her naïve question, I stumbled. Was Lady Gabriella so innocent that she didn't know how to pretend to fancy a man? Hadn't she witnessed other women flirting, even if she'd never done so herself?

I was tempted to tease her by encouraging her to express lavish compliments or use other such feminine wiles. But I wasn't at court, and this was certainly no game we were playing.

"Perhaps," I replied, "if we work near each other and engage in conversation, that will suffice."

She angled her head at me. "Very well. I shall endeavor to do so."

"Endeavor? Let us hope my company isn't overly distasteful."

Standing at the ladder protruding from the top of the hatch, she smiled, then bit off another piece of roll, effectively hiding all traces of humor. She tucked the leftover wedge into her pocket before she descended into the shaft.

I watched her climb down, and for the first time since arriving, I found myself eager for the long day of work ahead.

Though Gabriella was impatient to begin her weapons training, I convinced her to delay a week until the other slaves had the chance to see us together and conclude we harbored mutual fondness.

Most of the time we worked side by side, close enough to converse above the pinging and tapping of

Beholden

hammers and chisels. The first day, she was reticent to share much about herself. But as the hours and days passed, she opened up and divulged more.

I learned that her father, Lord Haleigh, Earl of Rockland, had once been an important advisor to King Alfred the Peacemaker. When the king had been on his deathbed and had divided his kingdom between his twin daughters, he'd beseeched Lord Haleigh to reside in Warwick with Queen Margery and advise her. Since Lord Haleigh already had a vast estate near the city of Kensington, he'd moved his young family to Rockland Castle where Gabriella had lived most of her life.

She'd been but a wee lass when her mother died giving birth to a stillborn brother. Crushed at the loss, Lord Haleigh hadn't remarried. But from how Gabriella spoke about her father, he'd been a devoted and adoring father, pouring out his attention and love upon his one remaining child. When I pressed her to tell me more about how her father died, she always changed the subject.

Of course, with her kind nature, Gabriella never talked about herself for long before she turned the discussion around and asked about my past. With the warnings about the volatile nature of the Great Isle and Queen Margery fresh in my mind, I'd hidden my true identity and told people I was a distant relation to Lord Kennard, that I'd fallen out of favor with my family, and as a result, I'd been relegated to work in the mine for six months as punishment.

To assuage my guilt for deceiving Gabriella, I tried to be honest in relaying all the other information about my family and my past. Leaving out a few minor details about my royalty and the Testing wouldn't matter, not in the long term when we parted ways.

Our charade seemed to be working, at least with Farthing, Ernie, and the other new slaves who jested with me mercilessly about Gabriella every night when we retired to our hut. And though I kept up the façade with them, I found it increasingly easy to do. The truth was, I enjoyed being with Gabriella. Her presence made me forget about the drudgery of the work and caused time to pass quickly.

The other truth was that the more I got to know her, the more concerned I was for her well-being. I'd tried again to probe into her situation and her unnamed enemy. When I asked her about the duchess's steward who had leveled the accusations of stealing against her, she'd offered little in her defense. My guess was that the steward had pilfered from the coffer to line his own pockets and had allowed Lady Gabriella to suffer for it.

How could I blame her for keeping secrets from me when I'd done the same to her?

"May I start training today?" she whispered as she stopped to wipe the sheen of perspiration from her brow. "Please? A week has passed."

I scooped up pieces of rock that had fallen to the ground and dumped them in my basket, bringing the level nearly to the top.

After pretending to be enamored with each other for the past week, what would Curly think if I pulled Gabriella aside today for a few minutes alone? Would he allow it? Or would he come after me the way he had the first day Gabriella and I had started talking? He'd pressed a sharp rock against my back and told me I'd fare much worse if I did anything to hurt Gabi, especially leading her on only to break her heart.

I glanced down the drift to where the leader and his

gang of loyal followers worked, not only filling their baskets but also completing quotas for the people in the infirmary.

There was only one way to find out his reaction. We had to sneak off.

"I'll go first." I tucked my tools into my rope belt. With my shoulders in a perpetual hunch and my head low to avoid hitting the ceiling, I crept toward the end of the drift, heading for a tunnel that had already been mined for anything of value.

A minute later Gabriella stepped into the passageway. She paused, uncertainty wrinkling her brow. "Do we have enough light here?"

It was dim, with scant illumination from the main drift. While it would be enough to hold any rats at bay, such conditions weren't ideal for teaching her how to wield a knife.

"We'll stay on the end closest to the light."

She searched the shadows, her fear palpable. "We cannot take long, so shall we begin?"

I slipped the knife out of the secretive sheath built into my boot. At the sight of the small but sharp blade, she blanched. She was the gentlest soul I'd ever met. I doubted she'd be able to kill anyone, even if she trained for it and tried.

"Take it by the grip," I instructed.

Gingerly she touched the ivory but then pulled away, biting her lip.

"Are you sure you must do this?" I asked.

She hesitated, then wrapped her fingers around the knife's grip. She held it awkwardly, and as I positioned her hand, I realized her training would be slow. Especially since her first and only lesson for today would consist of becoming comfortable touching the weapon.

If nothing else, my lessons would teach her self-defense. With a sharp rock, she might be able to protect herself if she were attacked again by rats.

Her knuckles were almost as white as the ivory handle.

"Loosen your hold a little."

For several minutes, she practiced moving the knife from hand to hand and getting her fingers into the correct hold.

"Good," I said as she gripped it tighter. At the crunch of footsteps nearing our passageway, I maneuvered her against the nearest wall and pressed into her, forcing her hand down to her side where the knife would be hidden.

She started to struggle, pushing against my chest.

"Take heed," I whispered. "Someone is coming." I nuzzled my nose into her hair and tried to act casual and yet ardent at the same time.

She sucked in a breath and held herself immobile.

I brushed my cheek against hers and was suddenly conscious of the softness and warmth of her skin as well as the silk of her hair.

As the footsteps entered our deserted passageway, she tensed even more. I dropped one of my hands to the knife and slipped it from her grip. I would be able to hide it up my sleeve until I had the chance to return it to my sole.

At a clearing throat behind us, I pretended to startle.

"My lady," Benedict said with a hint of anxiety in his voice. "Are you in trouble?"

"No trouble, Benedict." Her voice squeaked.

I quickly backed away, hiding the knife at the same time.

"We were just talking." She smoothed her hands over her stained skirt, even as a flush climbed up her cheeks.

"Were we not?"

"Yes. And now we must return to work."

As I passed Benedict, I could sense the disapproval in his gaze following me until I was gone. But strangely, all I could think about as I returned to my digging was the brief contact I'd had with Gabriella and the sweetness of holding her, if only for a few seconds.

Chapter 6

Gabriella

"Is she any better this morn?" Molly knelt across from me in the infirmary.

I let my song, one of the psalms, fade to silence before I pressed the cold cloth to Alice's forehead, willing her my strength and health. But to no avail. Nothing I'd done had helped my dear old servant.

"She still languishes with fever." I kissed Alice's cheek, the flesh hanging loose and lifeless.

"I'm sorry, Gabi." Molly hugged her shawl tightly, covering the stump still bandaged but beginning to heal.

At the rapid rise and fall of Alice's chest, I sat back on my heels, tears stinging my eyes at the helplessness of my situation. Back at Rockland, I would have had access to the apothecary for fever-reducing remedies. But here . . . in this godforsaken place?

If only we knew what caused the fevers. Some believed the superstitions, blaming wraiths for breathing upon some and not others. I suspected the noxious fumes that existed in parts of the mine had something to do with people falling ill. Regardless, I needed to find a way to bring Alice's fever down.

My gaze strayed outside to where a few of the overseers were finishing repairs to the suspension bridge so the supply transports could cross more safely. Was it possible I could plead with them for medicine?

Some of the women were laundering blankets and clothing on our one day off a week. Water bubbled in pots hanging over the central fire pit, lines were strung between the huts, and a few dripping garments flapped in the breeze. After the long winter months, our linens were in sore need of cleaning. But I couldn't leave Alice's side. I'd even skipped going down into the mines yesterday so I could tend to her.

I'd been surprised when Vilmar had surfaced at dusk not only with his bucket, but mine and Alice's, both full. He claimed others had done what they could to help, but Benedict later informed me that Vilmar had done most of the drilling himself, working without a break for hours.

I'd only spoken with Vilmar briefly when he stopped in the infirmary to deliver the food rations he'd earned for us. Later, Curly brought me the news that Vilmar and Ty had gone back down into the mine pits and hadn't come back up before the hatch had been closed for the night.

No one knew what had possessed Vilmar and his companion to descend or why they hadn't returned. I'd tossed and turned all night, thinking about what might have happened. And earlier at Mass, I'd offered prayers for him and Ty when I wasn't praying for Alice.

"Has he come up yet?" I asked.

Molly hesitated, her expression grave. Then she shook her head.

She didn't need to question who I was referring to. I'd playacted well during the past two weeks, convincing most everyone I had romantic inclinations for Vilmar. The only one I'd been honest with was Benedict. After his disapproval with the first training, I'd informed him that Vilmar and I weren't sharing affections, that instead he was teaching me self-defense, which was partly true. Although Benedict still frowned upon me going off with the handsome nobleman, he'd agreed to it as long as either he or Alice could act as a chaperone in the connecting passageway.

"Curly and the others are back."

"And they did not find any signs of them?"

Again, Molly hesitated. "No."

I couldn't keep my breath from deflating and my shoulders from sagging. Curly, Farthing, and a few others had descended earlier to search, and my worry had mounted with each passing hour they'd been gone.

I would have been worried no matter who'd gotten lost or trapped in the mines—at least, that's what I'd been telling myself. But all morning, I'd relived the way Vilmar's cheek had felt against mine on that first day of training when he'd pressed against me. My heart pattered faster every time I thought about his whisper tickling my ear or his face burrowing into my hair. On the couple of occasions we'd trained again, I'd anticipated having another such moment and was surprised by my mounting disappointment each time he kept his distance.

"What do you think happened?" I didn't really want an answer, since the possibilities were too discouraging.

"I'm sure they'll be just fine." Molly's tone lacked conviction. "Now, how about if you get some rest while I watch Alice?"

At the mention of rest, the exhaustion I'd been holding at bay hit me with the force of a winter storm. My eyelids drooped, my vision turned hazy, and I wasn't sure I had the fortitude to push myself up from the ground. Part of me wanted to curl up next to Alice, go to sleep, and never wake up to the nightmare of my new life.

However, I had to stay steadfast. I rose to my feet, refusing to let my body succumb to the weakness and fatigue that had become my constant companions of late.

"Thank you, Molly. You are a dear."

"You're the dear. You're the one always taking care of everyone else and never thinking of yourself."

I shook my head. "'Tis nothing more than anyone else would do—"

At a commotion from outside, I crossed to the door and exited into the warm sunshine. For a moment the light blinded me, but then as my vision cleared, my pulse halted. Vilmar stood by the hatch with Ty next to him.

Frantically, I scanned their bodies, searching for evidence of any harm. While they appeared pale and weary, they had sustained no bites, blood, or even scratches.

Vilmar was speaking with Curly as well as the others flocking around him. I had the strange urge to run to him and wrap my arms around him. But I refrained and, instead, sagged against the hut.

After several more moments of conversation, Vilmar shifted and glanced around the town. His gaze alighted first on my hut before it moved to the center fire pit and then to the infirmary. Was he searching for me?

My heart gave an unexpected thump of anticipation.

A second later his sights landed upon me, and my pulse thudded harder with a need I didn't understand.

He broke away from the group and stalked toward me. With his broad shoulders and bulging arms, his strength radiated from each long stride. His long hair had come loose and now flowed in the breeze, the sunlight highlighting hints of light brown mixed in with the dark.

I pushed away from the wall and straightened. Again, I had the urge to cross toward him, throw myself at him, and weep with relief.

As he neared, I clasped my hands together to prevent myself from such a display. Even so, I couldn't keep my voice from shaking as I spoke. "Where have you been? We've been worried."

He didn't say anything. But his crystal-blue eyes seemed to say everything. That he cared, that he hadn't meant to worry me, and that he wanted to see me more than anyone else there.

When he stopped in front of me, his brow narrowed. "Alice?"

"She's worse." The words emerged on the edge of a sob, one I rapidly stuffed away. I couldn't afford to lose control now.

Without averting his gaze from mine, he lowered himself to one knee before me.

My breath snagged. What was he doing?

He stretched out a fisted hand. "This is for you, my lady." As he unfurled his fingers to reveal a red stone, I gasped along with the others who'd followed Vilmar and now clustered around us.

"A ruby?" I whispered, hardly daring to say the word for fear it might disappear.

He nodded.

"How?"

"Ty found a promising old vein. We traced it to an area that hadn't been excavated, and then we dug all night." The crinkling at the corners of his eyes showed his exhaustion, and yet he held his hand out to me, unwavering.

At the silence—almost reverence—of the people around us, I reached out and touched the gem. While it was still encased in rough granite, the deep red gleamed in the sunlight. The coveted jewel could buy so many necessities from the overseers, things Vilmar and Ty could use, especially more food.

"'Tis yours." I retracted my hand. "I cannot take it."

"I found it for you. For Alice."

"For Alice?"

He nodded.

My throat constricted, and hot tears burned the backs of my eyes. How could I turn down this gift? The medicine I could purchase with it might very well save Alice's life. I touched the stone again, and this time he pressed it into my palm, giving me no choice but to take it.

As I held and marveled over it, he rose. Before he

could step away, I threw my arms around him. "Thank you."

I would have released him, except his arms wrapped around me in return, drawing me close.

Though I knew I should resist further contact, I surrendered to the sweet comfort of his embrace. As I pressed my face into his tunic, I breathed deeply, feeling both his strength and tenderness encompassing me. Somehow I felt safe and cherished in a way I hadn't experienced since I'd learned of my father's death.

I didn't want to leave his hold, could have allowed myself to stay here all day. But at the murmuring of voices around us, I peeled my arms away and stepped back.

Within seconds, the men were slapping Vilmar's back, congratulating him, and praising him all at once. As more people surrounded and separated us, his beautiful eyes held mine a moment longer, beseeching me.

For what, I knew not. When I offered him a smile of gratitude, his eyes lit and his lips turned up in a return smile. And somehow I understood that my smile—my happiness—was what he'd wanted in payment, that it was all he would ask for.

I let my smile widen. I could give him nothing less.

VILMAR

I was tired beyond endurance, but I slept fitfully the rest

of the day, my dreams filled with Gabriella at each turn. In every instance, I found myself first captured by her stunning gaze, unable to break free. And then in the next moment, she was in my arms, and I couldn't let her go.

When I awoke with a start, dusk was beginning to settle. Ty was still sleeping, but I knew at my slightest movement, he'd awaken and be alert to my every move. Though I'd been irritated with his constant hovering these past weeks, I was grateful nonetheless for his help in finding the viable vein that led us to the ruby. Without his aid, I would have dug all night for naught.

Be slave of all. The command and foundation of my Testing was never far from my mind. Surely I'd been sent to be a slave in the Gemstone Mountains so I could learn to serve others. And descending into the mine pits to find a rare jewel that could be traded for medicine counted toward that lesson, didn't it?

Despite trying to convince myself that my motives in searching for the jewel were noble, deep down I knew I'd done it for Gabriella, because I didn't want to see her suffer the loss of the maidservant she loved.

"I realize I've moved outside the bounds of the Testing," I'd said to Ty as we chipped away the stone, our hands blistered and our backs aching. "But I thank you for your willingness to aid me nevertheless."

He gave a weary nod, too tired for words.

"Next time we descend, I shall work for your rations."

"No. No need," he managed.

Now, his journal along with his pen and ink pot lay abandoned by his side. As I rose to my elbows, I was tempted to read the words he'd carefully penned there— apparently before allowing himself to fall asleep. What had he reported about my activities of the previous night?

If only he hadn't written anything.

Already, I guessed the Lagting would be none too pleased when they read Ty's account of my going off with Gabriella. Thus, I'd explained to Ty the true nature of my agreement with her. I hadn't wanted him to think I was trifling with the noblewoman or romantically involved. I certainly couldn't have him conveying such details in the journal and misinforming the Lagting.

But how could I explain the shift I sensed between Gabriella and myself? After spending so much time together, it was only natural we were becoming friends. But was our pretense turning into more?

I sat up and rubbed a hand across my eyes. The last thing I wanted to do was unintentionally lead Gabriella to believe something more permanent could ever exist between us.

Perhaps I shouldn't have gone back to seek a jewel. And yet how could I have done anything less? It wasn't in my nature to stand helplessly by while someone suffered.

I peered at the open journal again, then pushed myself up so I wouldn't give way to the temptation to read it. Even as I combed my hair with my fingers and tied it back with my leather strip, I feared that with each passing day, Ty's account of my activities was making me look less worthy of becoming the next king of Scania and not more. I had to prove to him—and the Lagting—I was serious about my Testing here in Warwick. But how?

As I left the hut, the other slaves stopped in the midst of their evening meal preparation to congratulate me again. Gone was the wariness and mistrust. Acceptance and warmth filled their faces instead. Even Curly nodded at me across the fire pit where he relaxed next to Molly.

I glanced around, hoping to see Gabriella, and

immediately half a dozen people directed me to the infirmary. Was my growing interest in her that readable? Or had our ruse already convinced everyone we adored each other?

Whatever the case, I should have guessed she'd be in the infirmary. That's where she spent the majority of her time. And of course, now with Alice having taken ill, she'd spent nearly every waking moment there.

Taking the praise in stride, I crossed to the infirmary and paused at the door. A soft melody wafted outside, beautiful and poignant at once. Gabriella had a lovely singing voice, and at times I found myself just listening, unable to interrupt.

With everyone watching me, however, I hovered only a moment longer before I ducked through the low doorway. At the sight of me, her song came to an abrupt end.

I made myself look at Alice, although I wanted nothing more than to take in Gabriella's beauty. The memory of her gratitude from earlier, the wideness of her eyes, the delight in her expression, brought a rush of warmth to my chest. And when she'd hugged me . . .

No, I wouldn't allow myself to think about her embrace, how she'd been the one to initiate it.

"How is Alice?" I asked.

"After I administered the decoction of yarrow and willow bark, her fever broke within the hour." Gabriella's voice was filled with such joy I couldn't keep from sharing a look with her. She smiled at me again, as she had earlier, and I knew I'd go down into the depths of the mine and do it all over again for that smile.

"She awoke a short while ago and had something to eat," Gabriella continued. "And now she is resting peacefully."

"I am heartily glad to hear it." Seeing that Alice was the only one currently in the infirmary, I wanted to sit across from Gabriella and simply be with her. Her gentle spirit had a way of soothing the troubled soul as much as her singing did. And yet, hadn't I just admonished myself to maintain better boundaries with her? After all, when I returned to Scania, the Lagting would finish making my marriage arrangements to a woman of their choice, likely a princess of royal lineage. Such a union would bring glory and power to Scania.

Gabriella brushed her hand across her servant's cheek. "'Tis my fault she is here. And I cannot allow her to die."

Some, like Curly, were strong enough to endure indefinitely. But from what I'd heard, most slaves didn't last long—maybe a year or two. Alice would be hard-pressed to make it through the summer.

What about Gabriella? How long would she be able to live in this harsh environment?

My stomach roiled at the prospect of her having to remain here for months, perhaps years, languishing until she was as haggard and maimed as some of the slaves who'd survived the longest.

Once I finished my six months of Testing, how would I be able to depart from this place, knowing how much she still suffered? In truth, how would I be able to leave anyone behind?

"I wish there were more I could do for Alice," I said. "And for you."

"You need not worry about me. I am able to fend for myself."

"Yes, you are indeed a strong woman." She possessed a reservoir of fortitude I didn't understand. How could she keep giving so much of herself day after day?

"If only I could find a way to secure a release for Alice and Benedict." She caressed Alice's cheek again. "They do not deserve to be here."

"Neither do you."

She focused on Alice, and for a few seconds I allowed myself the pleasure of taking in Gabriella's beauty—the soft red of her hair, the elegance of her features, the sweetness that emanated from her.

When she peeked at me a moment later, I dropped my attention to Alice.

"Vilmar," she said hesitantly. "When you finish serving your sentence, will you find a way to help Alice and Benedict?"

Of course she wasn't asking for herself. She was too selfless to do so. But I knew with sudden clarity that once my time here was over, I would make an effort to secure Gabriella's release. If I didn't try something, I'd never be able to return to Scania in peace. "I shall do my best to find a way to free you and Alice and Benedict."

"So long as Alice and Benedict are safe, 'tis all that matters."

It wasn't all that mattered to me. I held back my thought, but as I left the infirmary a few minutes later, I wished I hadn't allowed myself to care so easily for the people here. This wasn't my country, and these weren't my subjects. I had no business interfering in Queen Margery's discipline of her people, no matter how unjust her methods were.

I'd do well to remember it.

Chapter 7

Gabriella

I swept the knife sideways, staying light and agile on my feet as Vilmar had instructed. Then I aimed for the imaginary target where Grendel's neck would be and stabbed hard at the air, picturing the vulnerable artery there.

"Better," Vilmar said quietly from behind me.

I lowered the knife, as our time for today had come to an end. The scant minutes we had were never enough, but over the past weeks of secret training, I'd finally begun to feel more comfortable with the weapon. And Vilmar's directives for how to fight, move, and where to slice for the most damage, had been exactly what I'd needed so I could kill Grendel before he killed me.

If only I didn't feel my father's disapproval every time I held the knife. And if only I didn't always hear his words about kindness being the greatest weapon echoing in my mind.

With only three weeks until the Midsummer's Eve

Choosing Ball, my time was growing short. I needed to write to the duchess erelong. When she read my note, I had no doubt she'd send for me, which meant I had to be well trained in wielding a knife first.

Though Vilmar indicated I was better, was I good enough?

Sitting on a stone near the bend in the passageway, Alice had leaned her head against the wall and closed her eyes. From the peacefulness of her breathing, I guessed she'd fallen asleep. Thankfully, after receiving the medicine, she'd recovered rapidly. While still weak and easily spent, she'd resumed her work in the mines, though we assured her we would fill her quota.

As I handed the knife back to Vilmar, I hesitated in departing. Perhaps I ought to extend the training to allow Alice a few more minutes to slumber. Certainly I didn't desire to linger with Vilmar because I longed to spend more time with him, did I?

I couldn't deny that over the many days of working together and getting to know him, I'd grown to genuinely like him. It was difficult not to. Not only was he ruggedly handsome, but he was considerate and helpful to everyone. And after what he'd done for Alice, I admired him more than any other man I'd known, perhaps even more than my father.

Nevertheless, I couldn't allow myself to care about him beyond our friendship. Permitting anything more was foolhardy when I would soon leave him behind and never see him again.

He returned his knife to the hiding place in his boot. "Perhaps I can make a target for you to practice throwing the knife."

"Will that help?"

"If you told me more about who you're planning to fight, I would know how to train you better."

It wasn't the first time he'd plied me for more information. Something within me wanted to tell him, especially with his light-blue eyes imploring—almost begging—me to do so.

"Please, my lady."

The gentleness of his whisper was almost my undoing, and I had to force myself to think of my father's death and the queen's part in it to strengthen my resolve. "I cannot speak of it."

His shoulders sagged.

The secrets I held deep inside suddenly flared, scorching me with their heat. I should so like to share the burden with someone else. But I'd held them close these many months and couldn't stop now.

"What more can I do to aid you?" he asked as though sensing my resolve. "Shall I instruct you on basic self-defense techniques you could use if you should find yourself without a knife?"

I planned to have a knife when I met Grendel in the arena, and I planned to kill him the moment he reached for me. But if something went amiss, I would be wise to have an alternative. "Very well. What other techniques should I know?"

"Perhaps some moves that would allow you to escape an unwanted hold?"

"Unwanted hold?"

"If you're captured and have no weapon for fighting, there are other ways to break free."

Since I would be a willing sacrifice, I had no intention of attempting to free myself. Even if I wanted to run, the queen made sure the fairest maiden was unable to. But I couldn't tell him that. For several minutes, he showed me how to use my elbows to hit someone, lifting them to shoulder height and then pivoting and using the momentum to strike.

"Now if someone pins your arms from behind"—he slipped his hands onto my waist—"you must learn to free yourself first, using the elbow strike."

Before I could protest, he'd wrapped his arms around me, pinning me in place. He was merely demonstrating, and yet at his hold, all thoughts of training fled.

"You must bend low and shift your weight." His whisper was near my cheek. The solidness of his chest pressed into my back, and the strength of his arms enveloped me so thoroughly I couldn't think or move.

"The goal is to get at an angle where your elbows are once again free to use against your foe."

Even if I had been able to think or move, I didn't want to. I wanted to stay right where I was.

"Bend, my lady."

I closed my eyes and relaxed into him, resting my head against his shoulder. "Like this?"

"No, bend forward." I could feel him draw in a breath as though to explain himself further, but then he stalled. For a moment, his body remained tense.

Finally, I felt an easing in his muscles. "Of course, you can always weaken your enemy's self-defenses. That works too."

"Is that what I'm doing, my lord?"

"Very much so." Though his hold had loosened, his fingers on my waist tightened.

At the pressure, I relaxed against him even more. "And am I your enemy, my lord?"

His chest rose on another breath. And when he exhaled, I could feel the warmth near my ear. "Your beauty most certainly weakens me. But you are far from my enemy."

While such an enchanting compliment might be new for me, from the smoothness with which the words had rolled off his tongue, I could tell he'd had plenty of practice in the art of wooing.

"How many other women have weakened you?" The question slipped out before I could stop it.

He dipped his head, his mouth near my ear. "Do I sense jealousy, my lady?"

I started to pull away, embarrassed by the truth of his observation.

A gentle press of his lips to my temple stopped my efforts and weakened my knees. I reclined against him again, a thrill whispering through me. He'd been right. I hadn't needed to force myself to like him. Not even for an instant. He was thoroughly likeable in every way.

"I can admit to enjoying the company of many a maiden in recent years," he whispered. "But I can also admit none have ever come close to affecting me the way you do."

"Many a maiden?" I didn't want to think about him with *many* maidens, and yet I couldn't keep from imagining women more beautiful than myself falling into his arms and under his charm. I shouldn't be bothered by such images, but strangely I was.

I bent forward as he'd instructed me and then used my elbows to slug him hard enough that he released a soft *oomph*. As soon I made the move and twisted away from him, I clasped a hand over my mouth, horrified at my outburst.

He grasped his stomach and bent over.

"Vilmar." I touched his back. "I beg your forgiveness. I did not mean to hurt you."

He remained down for several more seconds before he lifted his head, his winsome grin in place. "That was just right. I see you are a natural at self-defense."

"Then you are unharmed?"

"No, I'm terribly wounded."

"Truly?"

"Wounded you think less of me for my past dalliances." His grin began to fade, replaced by a look I couldn't interpret but that made my stomach flip upside down.

"I do not think less of you," I admitted softly. "If you must know, I admire you most exceptionally."

"I admire you too, Gabriella. Very much." I could sense he wanted to say more, but at a noisy yawn behind us, I spun to find Alice was awake, watching our interaction without a trace of sleepiness to her countenance.

Had she been alert the whole time and merely resting? Had she witnessed me practically throwing myself into Vilmar's arms? If so, she would have seen I wasn't pretending to like him, that my attraction was genuine. Surely she would scold me later for allowing anything to develop between us when such a relationship was futile.

"Come now." I crossed to Alice. "We have been gone long enough and must return to work before our friends start to worry what has become of us."

As I helped Alice up and led her forward, I could

feel Vilmar's gaze trailing me. I forced myself to keep going, unwilling to look back at him. I'd already so foolishly revealed just how smitten I was with him. What good could come of allowing more feelings to develop between us when in three weeks, I'd likely be dead?

Hours later, as we began the arduous trek out of the mine pits, Curly fell into step behind me.

"I want ye to marry Vilmar," my friend whispered.

The words were so unexpected that I tripped and would have fallen except that Benedict held out a steadying hand.

"Marry?" I squeaked.

"Aye, marry."

"Hush." I glanced to the rear of the group, where Vilmar hiked with Ty. Hopefully, he was too far back to have heard Curly. Even so, the stone passageway was narrow, and every sound echoed.

"He be a good man and a good fit for ye."

"I have no plans to wed." I shifted my bucket from one arm to the other, the weight bending me over as it did everyone else.

"Ye must, so when he's done serving his six months and his family releases him, he can be taking ye with him."

"No one ever leaves the mine pits."

"Ye will. With him."

I climbed for several more paces, trying to process Curly's words. Was he insinuating I use Vilmar to escape back to civilization? And was such a thing even possible? Would the overseers and guards allow me to go with him if we were husband and wife? They liked me well enough that they just might. And would they let Alice and Benedict accompany me?

The very idea that I might be able to save Alice and Benedict from this nightmare sparked hope inside me. I'd already asked Vilmar to help free my faithful servants once he was restored to his family. And though he told me he'd try, we both knew he had no guarantees. Would the chances be greater if I married him?

Though I didn't know much about where he planned to live, I could beseech him to take us somewhere far away from Queen Margery and her cruelty and evil practices, someplace safe where she'd never find us.

But if I did so, I'd have to abandon my chance to put an end to the yearly sacrifice to the terrible beast. And I couldn't do that, not when I could save countless young women in the years to come, and not when I had the chance of bringing slavery in the mine pits to an end. Without the maidens, no more jewels would grow, and the slaves wouldn't be needed.

"I cannot," I whispered to Curly.

"Ye can and ye will." His voice turned hard, a tone I'd heard him take with others when he was determined to get his way. But he didn't know my plans to bring an end to Warwick's most dreaded custom.

"I shall not use him."

"Ye'll not be using when he cares about ye like he does."

My thoughts returned to earlier when we'd been training and he'd held me as though he cherished me. The remembrance of his arms surrounding me warmed my insides, and I still felt the imprint of his lips against my head.

"And ye cannot deny ye care about him in return."

Of course I couldn't deny it, not after the past few weeks of keeping up our charade. Even without the pretense, I couldn't deny I liked him. I hadn't been lying when I admitted I admired him exceptionally. It was the truth. Even so, marriage wasn't the answer.

"We cannot get married, Curly."

"People get married all the time in Slave Town. In fact, I'm planning to ask Molly to marry me erelong"

For a short while, I distracted Curly with talk of his plans to propose to Molly. But my redheaded friend was persistent, and I wasn't surprised when he brought it up again as we climbed up the hatch. "Ye don't deserve to be here, Gabi. And if ye marry him, ye'll be set free."

None of us deserved to be working as slaves in the mine pits. But I couldn't argue with Curly. Not when he only had my best interests at heart. "I shall think about it." Even as I conceded to him, I knew I would never take the easy way out of the mines, no matter how appealing the option might be.

Chapter 8

VILMAR

THE FIRE AT THE CENTER OF TOWN CRACKLED, SENDING SPARKS into the night. The flames leapt high, illuminating the flush on Gabriella's face as she twirled in a simple folk dance with the other women. A slight smile graced her lips, and her eyes shone with delight. With her long hair unbound and glimmering a pale auburn in the firelight, her beauty took my breath away.

"Ye love her." Curly's statement was low and certain from beside me.

I hadn't known he was there, had been too focused on Gabriella to pay attention to anything else. In fact, since the lute music had started at dusk and Gabriella had pulled me into the first dance, I hadn't thought of much else besides her.

"I don't know the folk dances," I'd said, as the others around us began to dance.

She'd tugged me farther into the fray. "Then it is my turn to teach you something." When she smiled, I hadn't been able to resist.

The dances hadn't been difficult to learn, and I'd found myself truly making merry for the first time since entering the mines six weeks ago. With the coming of warmer air and the lengthening of daylight, more people congregated outside in the evenings after we returned from the mine. Thankfully, the overseers didn't seem to care what we did, so long as we didn't cause disorder.

With a day of rest on the morrow, there was less urgency to retire to our huts and more freedom to take the little pleasures we had amidst the drudgery of slavery, and the pleasure of this eve was one I would not soon forget—especially the images of Gabriella's happiness in the dancing.

"Ye love her," Curly said again, louder.

I glanced around to see who might have heard him, but Farthing, Ernie, and the others were laughing and talking amongst themselves, oblivious to Curly's bold declaration. Only Ty, two steps away, glanced at me, as though gauging my reaction.

How exactly was I supposed to react? Of course I'd grown to care about Gabriella more than I'd wanted, more than I'd thought possible. Holding her in my arms last week during our training had left me shaken and filled me with longings I'd tried hard to forget. And I'd been afraid that if I touched her again, no matter how innocently, I would stir up desires that needed to remain dormant.

The simple truth was, I was not free to love her, and I couldn't give her that hope nor could I give it to Curly. I shook my head. "It's too soon to speak of love."

"It's been long enough for me to see that ye be the right match."

"I didn't come to the mine to fall in love."

"Nobody comes here expecting much of anything but pain and death. So if ye be one of the lucky ones who finds a jewel amidst the rubble, then ye best not be squandering your treasure."

The words were profound, and I couldn't keep from meeting his gaze and seeing the sincerity in the depths of his eyes. I'd long since learned from Gabriella that Curly had once been a huntsman for Queen Margery, providing game for the royal household from the vast forests surrounding Kensington. Last summer, he'd been part of the hunting party with the queen's daughter that had resulted in the princess suffering a fatal riding accident.

While the princess's death hadn't been anyone's fault, the queen still condemned Curly and two other huntsmen to life sentences in the mine. He'd survived nearly a year. But how much longer would he last?

Just this week he'd asked Molly to marry him. And from the tender way he watched his betrothed all evening, he'd found a jewel of his own amongst the rubble of his life.

"Gabriella is indeed a rare gem," I conceded. "You are not wrong about that. But I cannot make promises to her I won't be able to keep."

"Aye, I've seen that ye be a man of honor."

Gabriella swirled past, only an arm's length away. I wanted to reach for her and dance with her again. But what good could come of it? I would only end up hurting her when I left. Where was the honor in that?

"Ye want to do the right thing?" Curly asked more insistently.

"Of course."

"Then be marrying her and taking her out of the mine pits with ye when yer sentence here is completed."

"That's certainly one way to ensure her safety."

"Aye, and I wouldn't be suggesting it if I didn't like ye."

I appreciated his paying me a high compliment, but he also didn't know what he was asking. As a prince of Scania, I had no right to pick my own bride based on feelings or whim. Rather, wise counselors put a great deal of time into seeking out the right bride, and I couldn't deviate from that tradition.

Thankfully, the dance ended before Curly could say anything more, and Molly whisked him away. As Gabriella approached and invited me to dance again, I held back, encouraging Farthing to take a turn instead. Though everything within me resisted letting go, I had to be careful henceforth. I was treading in dangerous territory in more ways than one.

When the dancers grew tired and the music ceased, some made themselves comfortable around the fire, while others drifted toward their huts, yawning with exhaustion. My conversation with Curly still foremost upon my mind, I headed away also, only to stop at a gentle touch to my arm.

"Will you not stay by the fire a while?" Gabriella peered at me hopefully. "It is too beautiful a night to be inside."

She was too beautiful for me to be inside. But I stuffed that thought aside. I had to endeavor to keep our relationship from progressing. I'd done a pitiful job of that so far, and now with Curly's entreaty to wed her, I had to halt any notion that we had a future together.

My mind scrambled for anything I might say that wouldn't be too hurtful. But what else could be as effective as the truth?

"Curly just tasked me with marrying you," I whispered.

"Thus, I'm inclined to think we've taken our pretense of affection too far."

She studied my face as though trying to see deeper inside me. "Have you no wish to follow through on his task?"

I tried to read her expression too, but if I'd hurt her, she masked it well. "You must know I regard you highly and consider you a true friend . . ."

"But you do not want to marry me?" Her question was straightforward, without any bitterness.

Nevertheless, I hesitated with my next response. "I'm not in a position to make promises to any woman, no matter how much I might have grown to care about her."

She was quiet a moment, then nodded. "You have summarized my sentiments exactly. Curly has tasked me with the same. And while I understand he is thinking of my future, I am not in a position to make promises either."

At her easy agreement, my ready response stalled.

"Since neither of us plans to consider Curly's suggestion," she continued, "let us put it aside and give it no more thought."

Again, I was speechless. I'd been certain my rejection of a future together would hurt her. How could she disregard Curly's admonishment instead of grasping a chance to escape the mine?

"Now, come." She held out her hand. "The night is still young. Let us not waste the beauty of it because of our fears of the future."

I could do nothing less than place my hand in hers. As she led me back to the fire and tugged me down to the ground to sit beside her, I couldn't fend off my confusion—and perhaps disappointment—that she'd so easily accepted my decision not to marry her. I'd expected some tears, protest, or even anger. But she seemed fine. More than fine, in fact.

Was she relieved?

I wanted to ask her more. But as we joined the others in conversation, I tucked away my questions for another day. Next time we met for training I would pry further. For now, I would do as she bid and try not to waste the small moment of beauty amidst the unending toil and hardships.

"Only two weeks until Midsummer's Eve and the yearly sacrifice to Grendel," someone said across from us.

Gabriella stiffened. While our shoulders weren't touching, we were close enough that I was keenly aware of her every move and breath, though I'd been trying not to be so conscious.

Was she afraid of Grendel?

I searched my mind for everything I'd learned about Grendel. In Scania we called men like Grendel berserkers. They were madmen who frenzied and raged with the strength and wildness of a bear. When having a fit of fury, such men became dangerous and bloodthirsty warriors known to bite their own shields out of rage, foam at the mouth, and howl like beasts. Some kings throughout Scanian history had enlisted berserkers into their armies because they were known to kill without conscience and could wreak mass destruction amongst an enemy.

As a peace-loving king, my father had banned the army from using berserkers and had attempted to eradicate them from the land, locking them up in dungeons for their own safety and the protection of the people.

It was said Grendel had escaped capture in Scania and

now lived in Warwick, coming out on occasion to terrorize the people and the land. Had the queen learned of a way to appease the berserker? What was this about a yearly sacrifice?

I wanted to blurt out my questions, but doing so would reveal me to be the foreigner I was. Instead, I entered the conversation with care. "I have no doubt Ernie can regale us with a story about Grendel, especially the one relaying how the sacrifice came about."

"Oh, yes." Ernie shifted his legs away from the fire and situated himself more comfortably, clearly settling in for a long story.

Gabriella, on the other hand, stirred as though to rise, yawning in the process.

Before she could move too far, I slipped my arm behind her and drew her into the crook of my body. "Stay a little longer. The night is still young."

At her own words coming from my lips, she stalled. For a heartbeat, I was afraid she'd go anyway. But then she leaned into me and rested her head on my shoulder. While she remained somewhat stiff, I was relieved she hadn't run off, although a part of me warned I should have let her go, that no good could come of holding her like this in the firelight.

I silenced the warning. After all, she'd told me she had no interest in a future with me. I had naught to worry about.

"Once upon a time," Ernie began with his deep storyteller voice, the one that oft kept us entertained during the long hours in the mine, "a young warrior by the name of Grendel was exploring for gold in the depths of a mountain cave with his brothers. Little did the brothers know that their digging had awakened the wraiths who lived in the heart of the mountain. Before they knew what was happening, the wraiths blew their poison into the brothers. From then on, the brothers turned into monsters."

In Scania, some physicians believed that those who had changed into berserkers consumed a rare mushroom that made them rage and have visions. But, of course, no one knew for sure the cause of their madness.

"For a time, the brothers used their superhuman strength to defeat armies, but eventually scorned by kings and generals alike, one by one they all died or were locked up until Grendel was the only brother left. Hunted like an animal, he disappeared only to come out once a year on the day when the sun reaches its zenith in the summer sky."

With each word of Ernie's tale, Gabriella grew tenser. I stroked her arm and could feel her try to relax again.

"At the beginning of Queen Margery's rule in Warwick," Ernie continued, "every Midsummer's Eve, Grendel would come out of his cave and stampede throughout the countryside, leaving a path of death and destruction in his wake, killing hundreds of animals and people. Not even the mightiest warriors in the land could withstand Grendel's rage to capture him. And every year after his rampage, he retreated to his cave home in the steep cliffs at the edge of Wraith Lake, where he hibernated until the next summer."

Wraith Lake? I wished I knew more about Warwick. But I'd never studied the country in great detail, never been interested. Now, after meeting the people and living here, I felt a stirring of compassion I'd never expected.

"Finally, after witnessing the needless destruction, Queen Margery decided to try to appease Grendel. So, when he came out of his cave and began to cross the lake, she was waiting with a gift for him . . ."

"The fairest maiden in the land," whispered someone in an ominous voice.

I sat up. Why the fairest maiden in the land? Why would Grendel want to kill a lone maiden? I almost blurted my question and would have surely given away my ignorance, but at Gabriella's sudden shudder, I rubbed her arm again and tucked her more securely in the crook of my body.

"In addition to a dozen sheep, a dozen goats, and a dozen pigs," Ernie said, "the queen offered the fairest maiden in the land. Legend says that the beauty and purity of the fairest maiden has tremendous power—even the power to tame the wildest of spirits . . . and so it did."

A sick weight settled in the pit of my stomach at the vision of the berserker, raging about and slaughtering not only the animals but a beautiful young woman. How frightening for the woman and how devastating for her family.

"Henceforth," Ernie finished, "every year, on Midsummer's Eve, the queen holds a Choosing Ball at the royal palace and selects a maiden to be given to Grendel. The sacrifice of one prevents the death of many."

Silence descended over the group remaining around the fire, so the popping of the flames filled the air. A dozen questions raced through my mind—foremost, why had no one yet captured and killed Grendel? Surely, while offering the yearly gift, an army of the queen's best warriors could lay a trap and confine the berserker.

Gabriella squirmed to free herself, yawning again. This time I didn't attempt to keep her by my side. As she rose and walked away, I could only think of what the other slaves had said about her, that she'd been known as the fairest maiden in the land. And suddenly, I was glad more than ever that she was in the mine pits. While this was a dangerous place, at least here she had no worry of being chosen as the yearly sacrifice to Grendel.

Chapter 9

Gabriella

"Please, Gabriella. Go up to the surface with the others." Vilmar didn't pause in his rapid tapping against the granite. Bent over in the tight space, his voice was muffled and tired. Ty knelt beside him, hammering just as steadily.

"No, I am staying this time. You are the one who needs to rest."

"I shall rest once I have the gem in hand."

In the low torchlight, my frustration mounted as I watched Vilmar work. "You cannot keep going without sleep."

"We're close to finding it. Are we not, Ty?"

His manservant nodded, his shoulders stooped and his face haggard.

The two had been laboring nonstop since the previous day, since Alice had come down with the fever again, as had another woman. This time the fever raged hotter with each passing hour, and Molly had stayed above today to bathe the women and attempt to keep them alive.

I, on the other hand, had abandoned all else in order to aid Ty and Vilmar in searching the new vein for a gem. I'd been praying Ty's keen senses would prove right once more and that we would be rewarded with another jewel to trade for medicine. But the chances were slim, and we were running out of time since the fever had spiked so quickly.

I held the torch above Vilmar and Ty, hoping for some sign we were close. But all I could see was the same granite we chiseled every day.

"Please, my lady," Vilmar said again. "You need rest too."

At his statement, I swayed from exhaustion and hunger. I hadn't slept much over the past couple of nights while tending the sick women. During the moments when I'd rested and succumbed to slumber, my dreams turned into nightmares filled with Grendel drawing nigh, wearing the bear head and brandishing his bloody swords.

I closed my eyes to ward off the images that were growing more frightening. How would I defeat the wild monster with one small knife? Even though Vilmar had done his best to train me, I still trembled more times than not when I held his knife.

I glanced down the passageway toward the others, both dreading and hoping to see one of the duchess's knights coming to collect me. With merely four days until the Choosing Ball, I'd expected her to send someone by now. She must have received my note, and she would most certainly accept my offer to take the place of her daughter Tilde, wouldn't she?

If no one fetched me by the morrow, I would have

no choice but to plead with the overseers to aid me. If I explained my plan, would they be inclined to assist my leaving? At the very least, would they convince the guards to allow me to cross the bridge without trying to stop me?

My nerves quivered at the prospect.

At a sudden rumbling and cascade of stones from overhead, I ducked and covered my head with my arms.

Ty halted his tapping. He placed a hand on the wall as though taking the mountain's pulse. His eyes widened, and he grabbed Vilmar. "We need to leave."

"No." Vilmar easily shook off Ty's hold. "I'm staying now that we're this close."

"The stone will collapse—"

Before Ty could complete his warning, the tunnel shook again, bringing with it an ominous crackling and crumbling. Vilmar glanced at his manservant and then at the low ceiling.

As a crack in the granite widened, I could only stare.

"Run!" Vilmar shouted.

Before I could move, larger rocks began to break and fall against me. I couldn't keep from crying out in pain. In the next instant, Vilmar thrust me down and spread out over me, the curve of his body sheltering me from the onslaught.

For several infinite moments, an avalanche of rocks fell and would have snuffed out the torch if I hadn't protected the flame by cupping my hands above it, regardless of the stones battering me. When silence finally descended, dust and debris clouded the air.

Above me, Vilmar groaned.

"My lord. Are you hurt?"

Something wet dripped onto my outstretched arm. Through the haze I blinked and saw a spot of crimson on my sleeve. Another drip splattered and then another.

Blood.

Vilmar was injured.

I pushed him upward, and he groaned again. Rocks clattered and tumbled from him. He'd taken the majority of the blows while sheltering me.

My pulse sputtered. How badly was he injured?

I twisted until I was free and, at the same time, lowered him to the ground. I raised the torch and assessed him. His eyes were closed, and his face was pale. A rivulet of blood ran down his cheek, likely from a gash somewhere on the back of his head.

A quick look around showed that Ty was unconscious and bleeding too. From where he lay, I could tell he'd tried to throw himself over Vilmar but hadn't succeeded in time. Rocks of all sizes littered the tunnel, but thankfully, it hadn't collapsed on us entirely.

On the other hand, rubble now blocked the passageway leading back to the main drift, and we were trapped. In order to free ourselves, we would have to lift the stones away one by one. If Vilmar and Ty were too wounded to aid me, I'd have to do it by myself.

What if I couldn't move the rocks? What if they were too heavy? And what if I couldn't escape this cave-in to make it to the Choosing Ball on time?

No, I couldn't think so negatively. I had to shove my fear aside. First, I needed to tend to Vilmar and Ty.

Then I'd work as best I could to clear a way out.

After lodging the torch into a crevice in the stone wall, I knelt in the narrow passageway next to Vilmar. I hesitated only a moment before I unbound the leather strap holding his hair back. Then I slipped my fingers through his thick brown locks and felt along his scalp until I located the slick spot where he'd been cut.

At the probing, he moaned.

I raised my skirt and reached for the edge of my chemise. Now frayed and gray, it ripped with ease. I bunched it and pressed it onto his cut. His eyes flew open, and he started to sit up. "Careful. You are injured."

He closed his eyes and fell back. "Are you unharmed?"

"I am faring well." Other than a few scratches and bruises, thankfully, I was uninjured.

"And Ty?"

"If you are able to hold this to your wound and staunch the flow of blood, I shall check him."

Vilmar's fingers fumbled as he pressed the linen to his head.

I crawled over to Ty and touched the pulse in his neck. At the steady rhythm, I released a tense breath. He was still alive. Probing his scalp, I found several deep gashes. I ripped more of my chemise and tied bandages around his head and one around a gouge in his arm. After arranging him carefully, I returned to Vilmar. Blood saturated the linen at his head, so I tore another piece of my undergarment and laid it against his cut.

Vilmar's eyes eased open. "How is Ty?"

"His injuries are worse than yours, but I have

stopped the bleeding."

"Thank you."

"I should be the one thanking you. If not for your protection, I would be hurt too." As I tied the new bandage around his head, his blue eyes peered up at me, full of concern. I loved his eyes, so piercing and yet so tender at the same time.

"Can you tell how much rubble is blocking our exit?"

Through the haze, I once again attempted to assess the tunnel. Our situation was dire. But I couldn't tell Vilmar that. "I am sure the others will be working on the other side to clear away the rocks and aid our escape."

"It's that bad?"

It would take us hours to clear a path. Before we were free, our torch would likely burn down to nothing and leave us in the dark as easy prey for the rats. The image of Molly's empty sleeve hanging listlessly brought a lump of fear into my throat, but I swallowed it. "I shall begin removing the stones."

Though his expression contorted with frustration, he didn't protest as I rose. He likely knew that every minute of clearing away the debris could mean the difference between life and death.

I bent and picked up the nearest stone. At the scrape of a rock next to me, I paused to see Vilmar hunched over and lifting away a large stone.

"Vilmar. You are in no condition to stand, much less exert yourself."

He swayed, and I grabbed his arm to keep him from toppling.

"Once I get moving, I shall be fine." He lobbed the

stone onto a heap near the end of the drift.

We worked for several moments in silence until he sighed. "Why? Why all this work in the mines when so few gems remain? It's such a waste of time, not to mention a waste of so many lives."

"The new gems grow again after Midsummer's Eve."

"Grow again?" He scoffed. "Gems don't grow again. Once they're gone, the mine must be abandoned."

"Then why have slaves mined the Gemstone Mountains for years and never ceased to find them?"

"Why, indeed?" He tossed another rock.

Did I dare tell Vilmar the dark secret that had been my father's undoing? The real reason the queen never ran out of jewels in the Gemstone mines?

I glanced at Ty and then back at Vilmar. I hadn't told the secret to a single soul, not even to Benedict or Alice. I hadn't wanted to put anyone else in the same danger my father had experienced.

Yet, if I failed to kill Grendel and so failed to put an end to the queen's evil tradition of sacrificing a maiden, then someone else needed to know the secret. Vilmar was a man of honor, and perhaps he'd find a way to kill Grendel in my stead.

Before I could quell my misgivings, I forced myself to tell him. "The queen has the white stone, and her alchemists have discovered how to use it."

He halted lifting another stone midmotion. "The white stone? For making gold?"

All throughout history, alchemists had been attempting to make gold. Recipes, secret potions, cryptic codes, and legends had been circulating for centuries. The white stone—also known as the philosopher's stone—was one such legend. In fact, some claimed it was the most important ingredient in the alchemy process.

Apparently, Vilmar had heard tales of the white stone. Did he believe in its miraculous powers? That it held properties capable of transforming the simple into the extraordinary?

"My father, as a close advisor to King Alfred, was present when the king gave the white stone to his daughter Margery and three keys for an ancient treasure to his daughter Leandra. With the white stone in her possession, Queen Margery became obsessed and called every alchemist and philosopher in the Great Isle and beyond to assist her in unlocking the secrets of the stone. And they have been laboring for years."

"And now they have succeeded?"

"They did not discover how to make gold. Rather, utilizing ancient formulas, they learned all the ingredients necessary to combine with the white stone to create jewels."

"Jewels?" His voice held curiosity and, thankfully, was devoid of further scoffing.

"Yes, once a year on Midsummer's Eve, the queen and her alchemists create the concoction. Then her priests bring a special golden box containing the stone and newly made concoction to the Gemstone Mountains. They descend into the mines and sprinkle the mixture throughout the tunnels. Weeks later, after the alchemy process works, the slaves begin to find the gems."

Vilmar worked in silence for a moment, his expression severe. Did he believe me? Or did he think

I was telling him fairy tales? The whole process seemed too mystical and magical to be true. And I wouldn't have believed it myself, except my father had stumbled upon the truth.

"Last Midsummer's Eve, my father discovered one of the secret ingredients the queen uses to mix with the white stone."

Vilmar gave me his full attention. "So she killed him for knowing the secret?"

"She killed him because he wanted her to stop. Or, at the very least, he pleaded with her to find a way to make the concoction without using that ingredient."

"What ingredient?"

Before I could respond, Ty's faint voice startled us. "A human heart."

We both turned toward him. Ty was watching me with new interest, as though he could see my deepest thoughts. The intensity made me want to shiver, but I pushed aside the urge. "The white stone concoction requires not just any heart. It requires the heart of the fairest maiden in all the land."

Vilmar would have straightened and bumped his head on the low ceiling, but he caught himself. "So, after Grendel kills the fairest maiden, the queen uses the young woman's heart in her alchemy?"

I wasn't surprised he'd connected the two and now prayed he wouldn't also figure out my plans. "Yes, after the slaughter and after Grendel retreats to his cave, the priests take the young maiden away to prepare her for a royal burial in honor of her sacrifice. During the embalming, they remove her heart, and except for the alchemists, no one in the kingdom is the wiser for the queen's cruel custom."

"Except your father."

My heart ached at the memory of Father's agony the day he'd entered the chapel just as the priests had removed the maiden's heart and were placing it in the gold box with the stone. One look was all he needed to surmise the secret ingredient to the alchemy process, and he finally understood why the Gemstone Mountains never ran out of jewels. He came home distraught, paced for hours, and then fell to his knees in prayer.

After rising, he took me aside and privately told me everything he knew. Then he kissed me farewell, hugging me tightly and telling me to stay strong. At the time, I hadn't understood why. But later in the day, when he was attacked and killed by so-called bandits after leaving the palace, I realized his confronting the queen and standing up for what was right had cost him his life.

I'd also since realized I was partly to blame for his quest to put an end to the sacrifice to Grendel. At that time, with my eighteenth birthday less than a year away, he'd likely been desperate to find a way to save me.

"So, the sacrifice of a young maiden to Grendel isn't necessary?" Vilmar watched me carefully, so much so I feared he'd see inside to the plans I'd been formulating ever since I arrived at the mines.

I bent so he could no longer read my face. "Grendel's rage must be assuaged in some way."

"That accounts for why the queen has given up capturing him. She has more use for him alive than dead. The madman provides the excuse she needs for killing a maiden every year."

"Though many knights over the years have offered to fight Grendel, the queen has fanned the fear of the people, reminding them of what happens if a warrior should fail to kill the monster, how countless more would needlessly die."

"She is crafty indeed. If I were king of this country, I wouldn't hesitate to put a bounty on Grendel's head and handsomely reward the knight who brought him to me."

I almost smiled at the confidence in Vilmar's tone. He had a good and giving heart, but what did he know of ruling a country?

"I would not wish the fate of being sacrificed to Grendel upon any maiden. But I'm glad it isn't you."

I could feel Ty's keen gaze upon me again, and I focused on the rubble and the task of removing the stones. I couldn't agree with Vilmar. With the knowledge I had, I was the only one who could put an end to the madness. I'd rather forfeit myself to do what was right than stand by and watch the queen continue her evil practices for years to come.

Even more, I wanted to avenge my father's death. The queen had taken an innocent man's life for the sake of her selfish gain. She cost me the one person I'd loved more than anyone else. And I wanted her to pay for it.

But I wouldn't be able to do anything trapped deep in the mines. First, I had to find a way out before the rats closed in on us. And before I ran out of time to make it to the ball.

Chapter 10

VILMAR

THE TORCH SPUTTERED, AND I HELD MY BREATH, PRAYING IT would miraculously keep burning even though only a blackened stub remained. The clatter of rocks was frantic, from my tossing and Gabriella's. We'd both worked for hours trying to clear away rubble in order to make a way out, but every time we thought we were close to breaking through, we faced additional rocks. Had the entire mountain collapsed in this tunnel?

Ty had attempted to get up and help us, but he'd only been able to work for a short while before he bent over, retching. Gabriella insisted he lie back down and did her best to tend to his wounds and make him comfortable.

Once in a while, we thought we heard voices and the clamor of digging from the other side of the debris. But each time we stopped to listen, eerie silence met us.

Beside me, Gabriella paused, wiped her sleeve across her forehead, and then wearily grabbed another stone. Though we'd each long past wrapped pieces of her chemise around our hands to protect them from the jagged rocks, blood still seeped through the linen from all our cuts.

I wanted her to take a break and rest, and was angry with myself that I had to stand by and watch her work herself to exhaustion. But if we didn't make headway erelong, our task of staying alive would get much more difficult once the light went out.

She swayed, and I held on to her arm and steadied her. When she stopped singing some time ago, I realized she'd reached the limits of her endurance, so I taught her a lullaby native to Scania. That had rejuvenated her singing for a short while before she lapsed into silence again, not even having the wherewithal to ask me how I knew the lullaby.

"Tell me more about your mother." I tried once again to distract her from the difficulty of our predicament.

"I am too weary, my lord." Breathlessly, she heaved another rock onto the pile behind us. "Will you not tell me more about the escapades you had with your brothers? I wish my own brother had lived. I am sure we would have been dear friends."

I'd already shared all my stories about our childhood adventures fishing, swimming, and hunting, though I couldn't tell her everything without giving away my homeland. I also couldn't tell her about our strict education and training regime in preparation for taking the kingship, although with the chances of our escaping the tunnel growing slimmer, I wasn't so sure that keeping my identity hidden mattered anymore.

At the prospect of failing to free her, I lapsed into frustrated silence.

As if sensing my self-loathing, she apparently felt it was her turn to distract me. "What is the first thing you shall do upon being freed from the mine once your sentence is complete?"

"I would like a feast with an endless supply of mutton and herring. What about you?" Although her sentence of slavery had no end date like mine, I persisted anyway. "What is the first thing you'll do?"

"I should like a warm bath with scented soap."

The torch flickered again, and I paused. "Your chemise, my lady. Let's burn it and give ourselves more time."

Without my needing to say another word, she ripped a strip and set it on fire. As we watched the dirty piece of linen flame and disintegrate, I knew we were only prolonging the inevitable clash with rats.

"Take my boots," Ty said weakly from where he lay. "The leather will burn longer."

I couldn't. Then he'd be without footwear for the duration of our months in the mine, especially if I couldn't locate any more gems for purchasing a replacement. I wouldn't make him suffer that way. But he'd pushed himself up and was unlacing a boot.

"No. Keep yours. I'll burn mine." I stopped his hand and gently pressed him back to the ground even as I tugged at the laces of my boot. But at the flare of the fire behind me, I spun only to find that Gabriella had set one of her shoes on fire while she dangled the other, ready to add it.

At the sight of her pale feet poking out from underneath the ragged hem of her gown, my frustration arched, causing the wound in my head to throb. It wasn't fair that she'd been reduced to wearing ragged clothing and shoes, devoid of even stockings. And now, if I couldn't think of a way to save us, she might be bitten by rats and lose her limbs.

Hadn't she suffered enough? "The duchess's steward should be languishing here," I spat the words. "Likely he took from the coffers and blamed you."

She paused, and her shoulders slumped wearily. "No. I took the coins."

"You did?"

"I took coins once a month, just as I always had."

Surprise choked off my response.

She offered a weak smile. "Yes, I am guilty as charged, and I did not deny it."

"Technically it belonged to you—"

"'Twas God's, and I intended to give it back to him by distributing it amongst the neediest of my people, as I did on every new moon."

As she resumed working, I could only stare at this amazing woman. I'd come here to learn to be the slave of all. And I'd done everything I could day after day to serve the other slaves around me, including Gabriella. But I clearly had much yet to learn.

Moreover, I had much yet to do. Innocent people like Gabriella were languishing and no better off than when I'd first arrived.

Had I somehow missed the true meaning of my mission?

While my thoughts rushed frantically forward, I grabbed the rocks and threw them away from the entrance, working even faster. As I clawed and dug, she did the same, only halting to add more ripped pieces of her chemise and her other boot to the fire.

The flames rippled and gave off a dirty black smoke that filled the air and made it difficult to breathe. Even so, we pulled at the rocks, hardly daring to stop lest we lose a second of precious light to dig our way to freedom.

At a rumble and shaking, I paused a moment before I grabbed Gabriella and pushed her against the wall. I stretched over her to shield her from the sudden shower of rocks that cascaded from the entrance, rolling and crumbling into our passageway.

"Ty! Watch out!" I glanced over my shoulder, assessing how I could help him without also leaving Gabriella unprotected.

Too late, I realized the avalanche would threaten our meager attempt to keep the light burning. A second later, stones and dust doused the fire, plunging us into blackness.

For several more seconds the rumbling continued, until only a showering of pebbles remained.

"Ty?" I called. "Are you safe?"

"I've survived," he said through a cough.

I sagged, my relief making me weak. "Can you crawl to us? We'll be safest together."

"I'll try." His reply was followed by the clattering of rocks as he moved.

Against me, Gabriella shuddered.

"How do you fare, my lady?" I whispered, even as I felt the warmth of her breath and the rise and fall of her chest.

"The light is out." Her voice filled with fear.

I reached down and loosened my knife from my boot. "If you stay behind me at all times, I shall be able to protect you from the rats"

"But what about you?"

"I'll be fine." Although I was quite proficient at using my seax, I'd never had to fight off rabid rats in the dark. I'd have to use all my senses to keep them at bay.

I started to turn, but her fingers dug into my tunic. "Vilmar." Her whisper wobbled. "You were right. I have quickly become enamored with you. And I do not want you to be bitten on account of me."

A fierce protectiveness flooded my chest. Curly's words from the dance came back to me. *"You love her."* Was it possible he was right? Whatever the case, I'd do anything to keep her safe, even if I had to sacrifice my own limbs to the rats to do so.

Her grip against my tunic tightened, pulling me closer still, and her lips brushed against my jaw.

The movement was likely accidental. In the dark, she couldn't see where I was. It most certainly wasn't a kiss. Yet, in the next instant, her mouth touched mine, softly, tentatively. At the sweet pressure, I didn't care if she'd accidentally kissed me or whether she'd done so purposefully. In this moment, which very well could be our last, I wanted to kiss her, to let her know I'd never before met a woman like her, that I adored her.

Additional rocks crumbled behind us, but I couldn't think of anything else but Gabriella and the meshing of our lips. I deepened the kiss at the same time she did, our connection growing more urgent, more forceful, as if we both knew this was the end and we needed to make the most of every second together.

"Make haste!" blared a voice I didn't recognize. "Break through the wall faster."

I could see Gabriella's beautiful face again, so close to mine, and I broke our kiss, hope surging through me. Light was coming from somewhere, and maybe we wouldn't have to fight the rats after all. She would be safe.

Bandaged, bloody, and bruised, Ty stood several paces

away, taking in my position against Gabriella, no doubt having just witnessed me kissing her.

Guilt rose swiftly, and I released her and stepped back. What had I been thinking to take advantage of her in this moment of weakness?

A moment of weakness. Yes, that's all it had been. We'd simply been two people taking comfort in each other during what we believed to be our last minutes of life.

Thankfully, Gabriella's attention was riveted to the growing hole and the light streaming through it, not upon my remorse.

"Gabi?" came a familiar voice from the other side. Curly. "Ye be there?"

"Yes!" She tiptoed toward the hole, standing on her toes to see through. "We are here and unharmed."

"Thank the saints."

"Stand back as we blast the rocks again," bellowed an unfamiliar voice that set me on edge. Had the overseers descended to aid in the rescue? Certainly not. They never came down.

I lifted Gabriella back into the crook of the wall and safeguarded her with my body as another blow rocked the cavern and crumbled more rocks. She held on to me tightly, but this time she kept her head down, as though embarrassed by the intimacy we'd shared.

She needn't have worried. I'd made a mistake and had no intention of repeating it.

When the dust and noise began to settle, she lifted her long lashes and gazed up at me shyly. For several heartbeats, I lost myself in the beauty and tenderness in the depths of her soul, and in spite of my resolve, I found myself fighting the overwhelming urge to bend down and kiss her again.

"Gabi?" Curly broke through the last of the barriers.

I released her, but somehow felt as though she'd captured and kept a part of me.

"The rats?" he asked, his tools outstretched as he glanced around.

"We were in the dark but a few seconds." Gabriella maneuvered carefully through the rocks.

His gaze landed on her bare feet and then on the blackened remnants of the fire, now mostly covered in debris but showing the burned remains of one of her boots.

"Stand aside," someone commanded from the opening.

Curly climbed farther into our drift, filled with more rocks and allowing little space to walk. An armed knight ducked through the opening. He'd divested his helmet, revealing a battle-scarred face framed by dark hair streaked with silver. A second and third knight followed him.

Their attention fell upon Gabriella, and they bowed.

"Lady Haleigh," said the oldest.

"Sir Lucan?" Surprise and happiness laced her voice.

"Yes, 'tis I, my lady." He kept his head bowed in subservience.

"But I thought the duchess condemned you and your men to the dungeons."

"She all too quickly realized she'd reduced her defenses to nothing without us."

I tried to follow the exchange and make sense of who these knights were. From what I gathered, they'd once served Gabriella and remained loyal to her after the duchess condemned her.

"They helped us clear away the rubble," Curly interjected.

"Then we owe you our lives." From the confident way Gabriella lifted her chin, I could envision her as the lady of her manor, leading her knights and earning their respect.

"They've come to be taking ye away from here." The adoration in Curly's expression matched those of the knights—and no doubt reflected mine as well.

"Praise be." I couldn't hold back my relief that she would soon be out of this pit and returned to civilization. It was much more than I could have hoped for, especially as I'd struggled with thoughts of what would become of her once I finished my Testing.

I expected Gabriella to react with a measure of gratefulness to the news. Instead, her expression was somber. "Does the duchess agree to release Benedict and Alice as well?"

The older knight nodded. "Aye, my lady. She will free them as requested."

As requested? Had Gabriella been in touch with the duchess recently to petition for the liberation of herself and her servants?

"Very well. Then I shall go."

Was there any question of accepting the offer? If she refused, then I'd make her, and I had no doubt Curly would too.

She stepped forward. "Let us be on our way."

Sir Lucan glanced briefly at her bare feet before he politely averted his eyes. "Your shoes, my lady?"

"I burned them to keep the rats away."

I quickly bent and began to loosen my boot. "You shall wear mine."

"No." She stopped me with a touch to my arm. "The

way is too treacherous."

I straightened. "You shall either wear mine, or I shall carry you to the surface."

"Neither—"

I scooped her into my arms. My motion was so sudden, it forced her to wrap her arms around my neck. "Lead the way, sir," I commanded her knight as I started forward. I needed to move with haste before Gabriella protested and squirmed out of my arms.

As if sensing the same, Sir Lucan nodded and ducked into the opening in the rubble, but not before I caught the glimmer of curiosity in his eyes. No doubt he was wondering who I was and what right I had to carry Gabriella with such familiarity. Under other circumstances, I suspected he would have challenged me, but he didn't want her to walk barefoot through the rocky tunnels any more than I did.

Though my head throbbed from my injury, I refused to slacken my pace as we traversed the winding tunnels. Curly aided Ty and offered to relieve me on several occasions, but I shook my head, unwilling to relinquish my hold on Gabriella even as I labored to carry her.

We didn't speak, but somehow no words were necessary. She nestled her head on my shoulder in the crook of my neck as if to relish these last minutes together before our farewell. Her fingers rested at the back of my neck and combed through my long strands of hair. The barest touch served to remind me of her lips against mine, of the moment of passion we'd shared. And once more I wanted to bend down and steal another kiss—although with great effort, I refrained from doing so.

I could no longer deny my affection for her. It filled

every crevice of my heart. She brightened the darkness of this place with her kindness and concern for everyone. Her sweet spirit made the difficult days more bearable. Her beauty made the bleakness fade.

Of anyone here, she deserved to be free. I lifted a grateful prayer for this rescue, that tonight she would be able to luxuriate in the bath she'd longed for with her scented soaps.

When we reached the final ladder that led to the surface, I had to release her. Placing her on the lowest rung, I watched her climb up, already feeling the loss of her presence. It was for the best. She was never meant to be mine anyway.

In fact, perhaps her leaving was better for my Testing. Henceforth, I could focus on proving myself worthy to the Lagting and my father. I'd no longer have feelings and thoughts of her distracting me. And I'd be able to put more energy into challenging myself.

Even so, as I reached the surface and watched her embrace and say farewell to person after person, a deep sense of loss stole through me, casting a pall over what should have been a time of rejoicing.

More knights waited and bore the official standard of the Duchess of Burgundy. None of the overseers or guards could question the validity of her release—not that any of them would have, not with how fond they were of Gabriella. Like everyone else, they smiled at her good fortune.

Though Alice was weak, Sir Lucan had secured medicine for her upon his arrival. During the long hours we'd been trapped, Alice's fever had broken, and she'd had time to regain some strength. Thankfully, she was able to travel, though I doubted she'd be able to go far without tiring.

When Alice and Benedict were safely across the bridge and only Sir Lucan and Gabriella were left, she hugged her closest friends once more before she approached me where I stood to the side with Ty. Still wearing our bloody bandages, we hadn't taken the time yet to doctor our wounds. I would have plenty of opportunity once Gabriella was gone. For now, I wanted to gaze upon her beauty for as long as I possibly could.

"My lord." She curtsied, revealing the worn boots Sir Lucan had confiscated from the storehouse.

"My lady." I gave her a formal bow, all the while wishing I could gather her in my arms for a final embrace.

"I shall never forget your kindness to me."

"Nor I yours."

"You are an honorable man, and I know you will eventually find justice and be restored to your family."

"Thank you, my lady."

She offered me a sad smile. "Though we only had a short time together, I do not regret a single moment."

Was she referring to the kiss we'd shared? I tried to convince myself to regret it, but the memory of it would stay with me for days and weeks to come. Was it possible, after I finished the Testing and became king, I might be able to see her again, just as a friend? "Perchance one day we shall meet again under more favorable circumstances."

"Perchance." Her tone was wistful.

Suddenly the thought of never seeing her again filled me with dread. "If you'll permit me, I shall call upon you in Rockland after my release." I didn't know what purpose that would serve. What could come of such a visit? Nevertheless, she hadn't yet departed, and I was already missing her and couldn't imagine going forever without seeing her again.

She dipped her head in acquiescence to my request—at least I thought it was agreement. When she lifted her head and turned away, tears glistened upon her lashes and melancholy filled her eyes. Deep, painful melancholy.

The kind that had no hope for tomorrow.

As much as I wanted to stop her and ask why she wasn't rejoicing in the freedom she'd secured for herself and her two faithful servants, I suspected her sensitive spirit was likely grieving for all those she couldn't liberate and must leave behind.

I stood silently with everyone else and watched her carefully step from slat to slat across the bridge. When she reached the other side safely, I allowed myself to breathe again, even if each lungful was tight in my chest.

She mounted one of the waiting horses before she turned and gave a final wave to all of us standing at the edge of Slave Town. As she rode from sight, I pressed a battered hand to my chest to ease the ache. Her leaving was for the best. If only I could convince my heart of it.

The other slaves dispersed to return to the mine pits and finish their daily quotas. I turned to go too but stopped at the sight of Ty staring intently in the direction Gabriella and her knights had ridden. His dark eyes were more serious than I'd ever seen them. Did he sense some kind of danger for Gabriella?

I fixed my attention on the path that led down the mountain, and I went back over everything that had happened since Sir Lucan had come for her. He was an honorable man. I'd seen that from the first moment I'd met him. He and his men were well armed and certainly wouldn't allow any danger to befall her during the journey ahead.

"Is she in peril?" I asked.

"It is not for me to say." Of course, Ty was refraining from involving himself, the way he was supposed to. Only this time I didn't want him to refrain.

"You sense something bad will happen to her."

"You know I must not influence you."

"This is different, Ty." My voice dropped low even as my anger rose. "Her safety is more important than the Testing."

He shifted to look at me and arched his brow.

"I care about her." I admitted to something he already knew, especially since he'd witnessed our kiss. "I will put my Testing on hold if need be to ensure she makes it back to her home."

He studied my face, then shook his head. "I have already done and said too much, and I must not interfere any further."

With that he limped away. I watched him, my frustration building with each step he took. Gabriella would be fine. Even if the duchess made life difficult, at least she'd be free, and I'd no longer need to worry about her facing danger and death at every turn.

I would have to be satisfied with that.

Chapter 11

Gabriella

By dusk we descended into the foothills of the Gemstone Mountain range. After the hours of traversing the narrow mountain trails, I was weary. I could only guess how exhausted Alice was as she slumped forward in the saddle in front of Benedict. The old manservant struggled to keep her from sliding off, but he was weak himself from the months of malnourishment.

A short while later, we entered a small town, and I insisted we stop for a meal at the tavern. Alice roused enough to eat but then fell asleep the moment she finished. Benedict began nodding off too.

At their exhaustion, I knew it was time to part ways and so secured a private room above the tavern for them. As soon as Alice and Benedict were slumbering, I slipped down the narrow stairway and approached the table where Sir Lucan and several other knights were sipping ale. The proprietor and his wife sat at another table with a few other customers, their loud chatter and laughter a welcome sound.

The room was dark with a cozy feel, lit only by the hearth fire and low candle stubs on each of the tables. The remnants of roasted game and rye lingered in the air. I could still taste the greasy pheasant leg and the thick, soft bread—a feast after the simple fare of hard rolls and fish we'd had the past months.

"My lady." Sir Lucan smiled and rose, as did the other knights, who were familiar but whose names escaped my memory. Their faces were flushed from the heat inside the tavern, though a cool breeze wafted in from the open doorway.

"I am ready to leave. With all haste."

As though sensing my resolve, he placed his mug on the table. "Tonight, my lady?"

"Now."

"I thought you wanted to give Alice and Benedict the chance to rest."

"They will rest, and I shall move on without them." During the long hours of riding away from Slave Town, I'd had time to consider all the options, and as difficult as it would be, I had to leave Alice and Benedict behind. "Would you be so kind as to have one of your men guide them to Deerborne to live with my aunt's family? There they will be safe from the wiles of the duchess."

And they would also be far away from me and unable to interfere with my dangerous mission. For if they had the least indication of what I planned to do, they would lock me away and keep me from it.

Sir Lucan's brow creased into worried lines. "Perhaps you should go to your aunt's household as well, my lady."

"Perhaps in time." I doubted that would ever happen, but I couldn't say so. "For now, I must make haste to Rockland."

Midsummer's Eve was only two days away. We had at least a full night's hard ride ahead to reach Rockland. Once there, I would need hours to prepare for the ball, as well as time to travel to the royal residence in Kensington. We had not a minute to waste.

"If you're sure, my lady."

My thoughts returned to Vilmar and the picture of him watching me ride away. He'd stood so regally, his head held high, his shoulders straight, his bearing so bold and strong. Even though I sensed his relief in my leaving, I also noticed sadness in his countenance, a sadness that pierced my heart with the knowledge we would likely never see each other again.

The truth was, even if I managed to kill Grendel before he killed me, the queen would find a way to destroy me, just as she had my father. I had no future, especially not with Vilmar.

Nevertheless, the memory of our kiss had burned within me during the many hours of riding and now filled me with fresh yearning. I hadn't meant to brush my lips to his, but the moment I had, I knew I cared about him much more than I should. The kiss opened up longings I'd been battling—the desire to be with him and have a future together.

Once again, I couldn't keep from hesitating in my plans to avenge my father's death. I didn't have to fight back and try to end the queen's evil custom. What if I ran away—away from Grendel, away from Warwick, and away from the queen's cruelty? After all, why must so heavy a burden befall me?

The questions tumbled through my mind, increasing in speed like an avalanche. Before the momentum could find full force, I picked up my feet and walked to the door. "Let us be on our way." I spoke the words with an authority I didn't feel but with the weight of the burden refusing to release me.

I was the only one who could stop the queen. Therefore, I must see the task through to completion.

Clenching my jaw to keep from contradicting myself, I exited into the night. From this point onward, I must keep my feelings for Vilmar locked away. To allow them out would only jeopardize my ability to carry forth with the sacrifice I must make.

We reached the edge of Rockland by dawn. As the glow of the rising sun skimmed the land, I breathed in the sweet scent of the bellflowers, daisies, and buttercups that bloomed in a profusion of colors, welcoming me home.

Spreading out for a league, the fertile fields teemed with the new growth of barley and oats. The hay was tall and willowy and would soon be ready for haymaking by the peasants who worked the land. Herds of sheep grazed on the gently rolling hills that surrounded the fortress that had been my home for as long as I could remember.

Built on the highest knoll and against the backdrop of the Gemstone Mountains, Rockland Castle was majestic and worthy of royalty, which was one of the reasons the queen had given the estate to the duchess after my father's death.

The many towers were crowned with conical spires made of red clay tiles. Atop the brown sandstone bricks that made up the thick walls of the fortress, the red resembled the rubies that had once been so plentiful in the mountains.

As much as I adored everything about Rockland and had many wonderful memories of my childhood there, my fondness had never been the same once the duchess arrived with her daughters. Even now, as I peered at the fortress, a heaviness settled upon my chest at the prospect of seeing them.

I set my shoulders and nudged my mount onward. As we drew nearer, the gate rose and a retinue of knights rode out and veered in our direction.

"The duchess has been anxiously awaiting your return," the lead knight called to Sir Lucan. "She expected you yesterday, and with the delay, commanded us to ride out and discover what had become of you."

Sir Lucan reined in his horse. "As you can see, we are here now."

The commander of the retinue halted, his eyes widening as he took in how ragged and worn I had become during my months in the mine. He tore his gaze away and searched the rest of our party. "Where are Lady Haleigh's servants?"

"They were too weary to travel at the pace required of us." I spoke before Sir Lucan could relay the truth. I didn't want the duchess to discover I'd given Benedict and Alice their freedom. I feared she would send soldiers to capture them and hold them as ransom to ensure I did everything according to her bidding.

"Very well." The commander dug his spurs into his mount. "Then let us report to the duchess at once."

We crossed the remaining distance to the castle, my muscles tightening with each step closer. As we rode through the portcullis and gatehouse into the outer bailey, guards and servants alike stopped in the midst of their morning chores to stare at me.

I hadn't looked at myself in a mirror since the day I'd left for the mine, and now with the reaction of the people upon seeing me, I dreaded what I would encounter when I viewed my reflection. Had Vilmar only been flattering me when he told me my beauty weakened him? What if I was no longer the fairest in the land? What if no amount of bathing and grooming could transform me back into a beautiful woman? If not, I wouldn't be chosen to face Grendel.

Upon entering the inner bailey and approaching the keep, I caught sight of a well-dressed man standing in the central doorway. For an instant, I mistook him for my father, and my heart gave a wild thud of anticipation. But as we drew to a halt, the man stepped out of the shadows. Lord Query, the duchess's steward and advisor. With a narrow face and severe expression, he didn't resemble my handsome father in any way.

Disappointment battered against my already sore heart. My father was gone and would never return. He was, in fact, buried in the yard behind the chapel, right next to my mother. And it was the queen's fault. All she'd done was cause suffering to my family and to many more throughout the kingdom.

Sir Lucan assisted me from my mount and led me to the keep. All the while, Lord Query assessed me carefully. I had no doubt the duchess had already discussed my offer with him and that he had, in part, been responsible for recalling me from the mine, just as he had, in part, been responsible for my going there in the first place.

"Lady Gabriella." He bowed low. "The duchess is eager to see you. But I'm afraid were she to look upon you in your current condition, she would send you directly back to the mine."

Perhaps she would. At least Benedict and Alice would be free.

"She has fully forgiven Lady Gabriella." Beside me, Sir Lucan placed a hand upon the hilt of his sword, clearly intending to fight for my freedom, although I feared he would fail as he had the last time and perhaps this time find himself languishing in the mine with me.

Lord Query waved a hand as though to dismiss me. "Of course she's fully forgiven. I was only jesting."

Sir Lucan didn't remove his hold from his sword. Lord Query hadn't been jesting, and we both knew it.

"I shall retire to my chambers," I said to Lord Query. "And when I am presentable, I shall request an audience with the duchess."

Irritation flashed in his eyes. Before he could remind me that I was no longer lady of the manor, I swept past him, my chin high and my steps certain. I would show both him and the duchess I wasn't sacrificing myself because I feared them. This was my choice. I was doing it for my father, for all the maidens of Warwick who had lived in fear for too long, and for all the slaves who remained behind in the mine pits.

Chapter 12

VILMAR

UPON REACHING THE SURFACE, I DRAGGED IN A BREATH OF FRESH air. My head still throbbed from the wound I'd sustained in yesterday's cave-in, but I'd labored non-stop all day anyway, especially because Ty had been too weak to meet his quota. I'd hoped by driving myself to exhaustion I could put thoughts of Gabriella out of my mind. But she stayed with me every second, making me ache for her even more than I already did.

I dropped our buckets of rocks to the ground and then straightened and arched my back, longing to hear Gabriella's sweet voice offering encouragement to someone. But only silence met me, a silence that had haunted me all day, not only down in the mines, but now here at the surface.

From the somberness of those leaving the mine ahead of me, I guessed everyone felt Gabriella's absence as keenly as I did. She had been a beacon in the darkness, adding joy and beauty to this desolate place. And now without her, we were hopelessly lost.

Next to me, Curly aided Molly to the surface, hoisting her heavy load. I lent them a hand, gathered my bucket along with Ty's, and stood in line behind them to await food rations.

"Even if she has to miss our wedding, she's safe now," Molly said quietly to no one in particular. But from the way she slanted a glance my way, she was probably trying to make me feel better.

Following Ty's strange comments yesterday after Gabriella's departure, my misgivings had only grown. And I prayed Molly was right, that Gabriella was safe.

"But what about the ball?" Curly slid the buckets forward as the line inched toward the overseers in charge of the storehouse.

"What ball?" I asked.

"The Choosing Ball on Midsummer's Eve."

As I remembered Ernie's tale from the night of the dance, my pulse began to thud erratically.

"No need to worry," Molly replied. "With how weak Alice is, they won't be able to travel fast. Upon reaching Rockland, she'll have no time to prepare for a ball."

Not only was my pulse sputtering, but my breath had caught in my lungs. "But what if she goes anyway? Even with the dirt of the mine covering her, she would be the most beautiful woman there."

Curly clamped my shoulder. "Spoken like a man in love."

Molly tried to smile, but it didn't reach her eyes.

Surely there was little chance of Gabriella going to the ball and even less that she would be chosen.

"I pray for the poor soul who's picked." Molly's smile disappeared, and she shivered though the summer night was warm. "I wouldn't want to face so fierce an enemy as

Grendel. 'Twould be horrifying to stare death in the face with no weapon."

Enemy. The word rattled through my mind and body, sending a tremor all the way to the marrow in my bones. Gabriella had spoken of killing an enemy. And now her words came back to taunt me. *"I must learn how to slay my enemy, or I myself shall most certainly perish."* When I'd questioned her about it further, she'd said she would face the enemy in two months' time. Had she been referring to Midsummer's Eve?

I counted back the days to the time we'd started our training. Had it been two months? I couldn't say for sure, since the monotonous days blended into each other. When she'd spoken of an enemy, I'd assumed she truly had an enemy, someone like the duchess's steward who'd accused her of stealing. Or perhaps an enemy of her father's who wanted her dead. But what if all along she'd intended to face Grendel and attempt to slay him?

Curly and Molly shuffled forward in line, but I couldn't move. Horror coursed through me and froze me in place. Perhaps she'd wanted to learn to wield a knife in order to kill the duchess? What about the queen?

But even as the thoughts sifted through my mind, I shook my head. Gabriella would never kill a living soul, not even her enemy, unless she had some ulterior motive.

"What is it?" Curly watched me, his eyes suddenly alert and his body tense.

I couldn't speak. Instead, my thoughts returned to everything Gabriella had said during the weeks I'd known her—how she'd asked me to help find a way to save Alice and Benedict with no thought to herself, how she'd so easily put aside Curly's prompting to wed me, and how she'd claimed she was in no position to make any promises.

Then just yesterday, when the knights had blasted us out of the cave-in, she'd mentioned petitioning the duchess for her discharge. Why would the duchess agree to a release unless Gabriella had struck a deal—a deal to give herself over to Grendel as the chosen one?

I cannot speak the name," she'd said. She hadn't been willing to tell me the name of her enemy because she knew I'd stop her. She knew we would all try to stop her.

From a place deep inside, a groan fought for release. The truth was, Gabriella had left the mine pits with the precise purpose of attending the Choosing Ball and attempting to kill Grendel. She was generous enough in spirit to make the ultimate sacrifice in order to bring an end to the terrifying custom.

"You look as though you've seen a wraith." Curly shifted my buckets and pulled me with them.

I peered through the fading twilight to the hut where Ty had disappeared. Had he guessed Gabriella's plans already? Was that why he'd acted strangely yesterday upon her leaving? If only he'd told me his suspicions much sooner, I could have done something to prevent her from going.

But would she have stayed? After all she'd revealed to me about the queen's alchemy and the need for the heart of the fairest maiden as one of the ingredients, I understood the reasoning behind wanting to stop the madness that had gone on for too long.

Nonetheless, surely Gabriella didn't think she could face a berserker with a simple knife and be able to kill him. I'd been a young boy when my father captured the last of the berserkers in Scania. It had taken a dozen of the strongest and fiercest knights to suppress the madman. Even then, after securing him within the confines of the stiffest chain-mail nets, several of the knights had lost their lives holding him down, and others had been wounded.

Against so fierce a foe, Gabriella wouldn't have the slightest chance of even getting near the berserker. He'd tear her asunder before she could take one swing of any weapon she somehow managed to conceal.

"Tell me what's wrong." Curly spoke more adamantly. "Has something happened to Gabi?"

"Yes. I have to go." Without wasting another second, I stepped out of line and started down the path. I didn't know how I'd overcome the guards standing at the bridge. All I knew was that I had to escape from the mine pits and be at the Choosing Ball so I could stop Gabriella from making a deadly mistake.

The crunch of Curly's footsteps chased me. I picked up my pace, but he yanked on my arm and wrenched it behind my back. The pain ripped through me and forced me to my knees.

"Let me go!" I struggled against Curly's hold.

He twisted my arm tighter and then bent and spoke low near my ear. "If ye try to escape now, ye will be caught and thrown over the bridge down into the ravine. Then what good will ye be to Gabi?"

I paused in my thrashing. He was right. The tower guards were armed with bows and arrows. They'd shoot anyone who tried to cross the bridge and would let them fall to the rocks far below. Though it hadn't happened during my time in the mine, I'd heard the stories of men who'd attempted to escape. None had ever lived to return.

Yet as far as I knew, none of them had a weapon to aid their efforts like I did. I jerked against Curly's hold. "I can make it," I said through clenched teeth.

"Nay, ye won't make it." His voice was as steely as his unwavering grip.

My desperation pulsed harder. "I have to try!"

"Ye will be dead before ye can reach a dozen slats."

Through the panic, I forced myself to remember everything I'd ever learned about hand-to-hand combat. With a swift jab of my free elbow, I took Curly off guard. At the slight weakening in his hold, I bent and flipped him over my body.

He lost his grip on me and landed on the hard, rocky ground in front of me. In the next second, I was on my feet and ready to flee. What I hadn't counted on was the other slaves who'd been watching our interaction and now surrounded us.

"Grab him," Curly growled to his friends.

For the first time since arriving at the mine, I was desperate enough to reveal my true identity as a prince and command them to stop. But the men were already upon me, leaving me with no choice but to swing and kick with all the techniques I'd learned during my years of warrior training. Though I was skilled, I was outnumbered, and moments later, several men locked my arms behind my back again and held me in place.

Curly stood and wiped the blood from a gash in his cheek. I was sorry for hurting him, but he was out of line in attempting to impede me.

Our altercation had drawn the attention of several guards and overseers.

"Take him to my place." Curly's whisper was urgent. As he straightened, he gave a curt nod toward the guard standing in the tower next to the bridge.

Only then did I notice the guard had trained an arrow

upon us. I ceased my struggling, having no wish to bring harm upon anyone. I didn't want them riddled with arrows on account of my disorderliness.

They dragged me to Curly's hut. Ty had joined the throng. No doubt he'd heard the commotion and come out to observe my newest escapade. I was indeed giving him much fodder for his journal. Last night, in spite of his injuries, he'd scribbled away furiously, likely detailing the account of our time trapped in the tunnel and revealing my kiss with Gabriella. Tonight, he'd relay my desire to escape the mine and go after her.

Though I'd vowed to focus more fully on my Testing now that Gabriella was gone, I couldn't keep from picturing her surrounded by dozens of sheep, goats, and cows as she waited for Grendel's approach. In light of her peril, the Testing no longer mattered. I didn't care about my future or about anything Ty might write down. All I cared about was getting to Gabriella before the berserker did.

The men forced me to the ground in front of the hearth fire but didn't release me. Ty stood tensely close by. Someone tossed fuel onto the low flames, bringing light to the barren dwelling and illuminating Curly's face. I expected to see anger, but his features reflected worry and determination.

When he lowered himself to the dirt floor across the fire from me, he finally gave me his full attention. "If Gabi's in trouble, then it's time ye be telling us all ye know."

My body protested being held. And yet now that I was sitting, a warning in the back of my mind shouted that I couldn't just rush off without coming up with a plan. Maybe Curly and these other slaves would even be willing to aid in my escape from the mine. Was it possible I needed them more than they needed me?

With the hazy smoke of the fire filling the hut, I told Curly everything I knew about Gabriella's plans. He'd already seen my knife, so it was no news to him that I had one. However, he hadn't realized I'd been using my time alone with Gabriella to train her how to wield the weapon.

I shared what Gabriella had told me about her father's discovery of the priests taking the young maiden's heart to be used as an alchemy ingredient and how the jewels began to surface once the priests descended into the mines and performed their yearly blessing, which involved sprinkling the concoction they'd made from the maiden's heart and the white stone.

The men listened intently, their unwavering gazes upon me. When I finished my tale, they were silent. No one moved. And surprisingly, no one ridiculed me.

"I suspect she intends to end the ritual once and for all," I said more urgently. "And perhaps she even hopes by doing so to stop the jewel production and the need for slavery in the mines."

Curly gave a grave nod.

"I must leave now in order to reach her by tomorrow's ball and stop her."

"She won't make it there in time," Curly said, as he had earlier. "And even if she does, she has no guarantee of being chosen by the queen, since only the fairest maiden can sate Grendel . . ."

I'd already spoken the truth to him when I told him that, even at her worst, Gabriella was still the fairest maiden in the land. Certainly, the queen would recognize that. And if Gabriella presented herself as a willing sacrifice, how could the queen turn her down?

The darkness penetrating the open door indicated I now had less than twenty-four hours to figure out a way to travel to her and convince her not to go through with her plans. And if she didn't listen to me, then I would forcibly drag her from the ball, lock her up, and then go out and kill Grendel in her stead.

All along, I'd been telling myself that because I was a foreigner, the problems of this country weren't mine to fix. And now, if I interfered with the queen's sacrifice to Grendel, I would be overstepping. The queen might arrest me and hold me as her prisoner. I could very well find myself back in the mine forever and not just for six months.

On the other hand, how could I sit back and do naught? If Gabriella was willing to sacrifice her life to bring about change, shouldn't I be ready to do the same?

Deep inside, I knew I could do nothing less. No matter the consequences, I had to do the right thing and put an end to the needless sacrifice, slaughter, and slavery the queen perpetuated. Maybe I even had a responsibility to do so. After all, Grendel was from Scania.

"Gabriella has already proven she'll do whatever she must in order to fight Grendel. I have no doubt she'll make sure she's chosen."

Curly stared into the dancing flames, his face rigid like flint.

I struggled against the men still holding me captive. "If you let me go, I shall seek her out with all haste."

"Ye cannot do this alone."

"Then you agree she's in danger?"

"Aye. If she be intending to do as ye said, then she'll find a way to be at the ball, even if she has to leave Alice and Benedict behind to get there."

"And if she leaves them behind," said another, "she won't have to worry about anyone trying to stop her."

They were right. If only Sir Lucan would intervene. But the knight had clearly been riddled with guilt for not previously protecting Gabriella. At present, he'd likely do anything she wished to make up for his mistakes, even unwittingly lead her to her death.

"How far from here to the queen's residence?" I didn't care anymore if I showed my ignorance.

"Twelve hours by foot and six or less by horse," said Ernie from where he stood by the doorway.

"Can you lead me there?" Ernie would know the best way in, perhaps even through the kitchen.

Before Ernie could respond, Curly shook his head. "Not one person has ever escaped from the mine, much less two."

I held back a frustrated sigh. "Then release me, and I shall make the escape on my own."

Curly continued to stare into the flames, a battle warring across his features. "I know the back trails through the foothills. And if necessary, I can lead ye inside the palace grounds undetected."

As a former huntsman for the queen, he would indeed know the way, keeping us far from the usual routes where we might encounter people who would easily recognize us as runaway slaves.

And yet, he'd just admitted the mission—especially the escape from the mine—was too dangerous. I couldn't involve him any more than I could Ernie.

"You will inform me of the way, and I shall commit it to memory." I hoped the authority in my voice would make him back down.

"Ye cannot fight the monster by yerself." His voice

turned equally hard.

"And who said I planned to fight Grendel?"

He met my gaze and held it.

"Even if I were planning to fight him, I couldn't ask you to join in."

"What if this is the chance I've been waiting for? The chance to redeem myself?"

Redeem himself from what? My unspoken question hung in the air between us as heavy as the smoke. But this was neither the time nor place to press Curly for more answers about his past life. We had more urgent matters at hand.

"Very well. How can two of us cross the bridge without detection?"

"We can't. I told you, it's never been done."

A slave standing guard outside the hut poked his head inside. "One of the overseers is coming."

At his hissed whisper, several lowered themselves to the ground and pretended to be asleep. The men who'd been holding me escaped out the back window, leaving me free to run away.

I could go right now and spare Curly. And what about Ty? If I left, he'd likely attempt to cross the bridge and put himself in grave peril too.

No, if I was going to fight my way free, I would have to do it alone.

Chapter
13

Gabriella

I knelt and kissed the duchess's outstretched hand. The jewels from her rings brushed against my face and were as cold and hard as her fingers. Without lifting my head, I shifted and reached for Tilde's hand. Although she allowed me the perfunctory kiss, she hastily withdrew from me, as if my touch made her dirty. Signe, two years younger, didn't bother to extend her hand and instead tucked both behind her back.

After spending the entire day and well into the evening doing my best to erase the past months of the mine from my skin and body, I still had more work to do before I would meet noble standards. I'd likely need to alternate between bathing and oil treatments for most of the coming night before I took my leave in the morning for Kensington.

The servants who remained from my childhood had been delighted to see me again. They'd paid visits to my chambers off and on throughout the day to welcome me home. Their tears of joy had been a balm for my aching soul, although the reunion was also bittersweet in knowing I would leave them again so soon.

After I departed on the morrow, they would realize all too clearly, if they hadn't already, the reason for my release from the mine—that the duchess was sending me to the Choosing Ball in Tilde's place. Every household must send their fairest maiden, an unmarried woman between the ages of eighteen and twenty. No one was exempt, not even the duchess.

"You may rise," the duchess said.

Sir Lucan at my side aided me up, and as I straightened, I was again keenly aware of how my beauty had faded. My hands were callused and my fingernails gritted with dirt that now seemed permanent. My red hair dangled in long waves but was coarse and dull. My gown, which had once highlighted my womanly form, now hung listlessly on my too-thin frame.

Did I have a chance of being chosen for the sacrifice? I held my breath as the duchess assessed me and hoped she wouldn't find me overly lacking.

The duchess would have to send Tilde if she didn't send me. And the duchess would do whatever she could to keep her daughter at home. After all, no young woman, whether fair or not, wanted to go to the ball and risk being chosen. In most households, the day before Midsummer's Eve was filled with great solemnity. At dawn on the day of the ball, the young women were ushered away with much lamenting, as if they were leaving for their funerals instead of the queen's festivities.

"The mine has not been kind to you." The duchess stood from the golden chair that had once belonged to my father. Inlaid with colorful gems, it was worthy of a king or queen. The entire hall was exquisitely crafted befitting royalty. From the colorful mosaic tiles in the walls to the dome overhead inlaid with gold plate and engraved with intricate patterns, my father had created it as a tribute to King Alfred and his family, hoping that when they visited, they would find it admirable.

On the few occasions Queen Margery had come to Rockland Castle, she always expressed her appreciation. But part of me couldn't keep from wondering if she'd been calculating how to do away with my father in order to claim the land and wealth for herself.

Of course, after my father's untimely demise, she'd been too diplomatic to swoop in and take possession of Rockland in her own right. As many of her council already suspected Father's death had been no accident, such a move would have placed greater suspicion upon her. Instead, she'd used the duchess as her pawn to oversee the estate while at the same time having access to whatever she wanted of my father's holdings and coffers.

A mocking smile tugged at the duchess's lips. With her dark hair swept up into a severe high coif that was covered in dangling jewels, her fleshy face was powdered into an unnatural white. Of medium height, she was large boned and bulky like her brother, Ethelred, who had married Queen Margery and seemed to love her ardently until he passed away. Their only son and the heir to the throne, Prince Ethelbard, was of stocky build, as was the young

Princess Ruby. Only the oldest daughter, Princess Pearl, had inherited Margery's slender beauty.

I'd met Princess Pearl during one of the queen's visits to Rockland. A year different in age, we'd bonded well. I'd longed to have her for a friend, but the queen had never allowed Pearl to return to Rockland. Early last summer, the beautiful young woman had died during a hunting accident.

Some speculated Pearl's death hadn't been by chance. They said that since Pearl had turned eighteen, the queen had staged Pearl's death and then sent the princess into hiding to save her from having to be sacrificed to Grendel. With her dark hair, green eyes, and flawless skin, Pearl had easily been the fairest maiden in Warwick. The queen would have had no option but to pick her own daughter at the Choosing Ball.

Other rumors hinted at more sinister reasons behind Pearl's death. Everyone knew the queen had been jealous of her daughter for outshining her in not only beauty but in charm and poise. The simple truth was that people liked Pearl more than Queen Margery. Some had even begun to proclaim that Pearl should be the next queen. There were rumors of rebelling against Queen Margery and making Pearl the next leader, even over Prince Ethelbard.

"I told you that you wouldn't be pleased, Your Grace." Lord Query leaned in toward the duchess and whispered loud enough that everyone near the front of the hall could hear.

"Mother." Tilde's voice wobbled, her eyes filling with tears. "You said I wouldn't need to go to the ball."

"And you will not." The duchess patted Tilde's arm,

her rings clinking together.

"But she's ugly, Mother. Simply deplorable."

"Of course, no one can compare to you and Signe." The duchess eyed me again critically. "But we shall do our best to make her presentable."

Tilde sniffled noisily, her face splotchy and her eyes red, likely from the worry of the past week of waiting for my arrival. I wanted to feel sorry for her and the distress I'd inadvertently caused her, but all I felt was emptiness.

When Tilde and Signe had first moved to Rockland, I'd hoped we could be like sisters. If nothing else, I'd been excited at the prospect of companionship, especially since I'd been lonely and missing my father. However, after the months of hurtful criticism and petty accusations, I learned my hope had been in vain. The Scripture imploring us to pray for those who persecute us had taken on new meaning.

The duchess lifted her chin, her flesh wobbling slightly. "Take her away and work harder to make her the fairest maiden in the land."

VILMAR

As one of the overseers stepped into the doorway of Curly's hut, I forced myself to remain in my place in front of the fire. I would have to wait to make my escape until after the overseer retreated.

The burly man squinted through the haze until he found Curly. "You know you ain't supposed to have gatherings of more than five."

"Aye, we know." Curly wiped at the blood still flowing from the cut on his face. "We be trying to calm Vilmar. He's taken Gabi's leaving hard."

The overseer's attention shifted to me, and he nodded, his expression almost sympathetic. I guess he'd seen me with Gabriella oft enough to assume, like everyone else, that we cared deeply for each other. "We'll miss her, aye, that we will. She was a rare jewel, that one."

"She was indeed." And now I needed to find a way to rescue my rare jewel.

Was she mine?

The claim had entered my thoughts unbidden. But once there, I couldn't dislodge it. We hadn't made promises to each other. In fact, we'd put all thoughts from our minds of a future together. Why, then, did I feel as though, in her leaving, I'd lost a part of myself?

The overseer leaned against the doorjamb. "I remember the time back a few months when good ol' Paddy had a heart attack and she nursed him back to health." The overseer seemed intent upon recalling each and every instance of Gabriella's kindness. While the reminiscing was a fine tribute to her memory, every minute of delay could mean the difference between her life and death, and I grew tenser with each passing moment.

Finally, the overseer straightened. "She'll be missed around here, that she will. But can't say I'm sorry, since she gets to be in a better place."

If only he knew the truth. A truth I wished I'd discovered long before now.

"See that you keep to the limit in here," the overseer said amiably. "Or next time the guards might insist we start locking you up."

While congregating outside was permitted, large gatherings within the dwellings were prohibited to prevent us from plotting rebellion. It was a foolish rule, since if we wanted to plan an uprising, we could do so underground while we worked.

I sat forward and didn't dare glance at Ty sitting beside me for fear he'd see my thoughts. *Plotting rebellion. Plan an uprising.* Was it possible for me to lead a rebellion here? Tonight? A bolt of energy raced through me, but I forced myself to remain as nonchalant as possible until the overseer sauntered away.

Even then, I stared at the hearth fire, a dozen plans formulating all at once, even in light of the tales of past failed revolts, of slaves rising up only to be slaughtered by the guards with their superior weapons and armor.

I certainly didn't want to put lives needlessly at risk. If such a rebellion was doomed to failure, I shouldn't even think about starting one. And yet, what if I could succeed and set every slave in this horrible place free?

My mind warred with itself. Already I was overstepping my bounds in planning to escape and kill a berserker. But if I led a revolt amongst the slaves in the mine pits, I'd be involving myself irrevocably in this country that didn't belong to me and in problems that weren't mine to solve.

I couldn't barge into Warwick's problems and assume I could make them better. In leading such a revolt and in killing Grendel, I risked angering the queen and making things worse for the people. I also chanced making an enemy for Scania.

I buried my face in my hands. I couldn't plan an insurrection, and not just because it might make things worse for everyone in Warwick, but because doing so would likely put an end to my Testing. There weren't many rules regarding our Testing, but one regulation was clear enough. If we abandoned our Testing, we would forfeit any claim to the throne. Of course, a provision existed for leaving temporarily. If we had to go away from the place chosen for us, at the very least we must return and finish the Testing.

But if I led a revolution and freed the slaves, there would be naught to return to. And even if the queen kept her mine operational after a revolt, how would I be able to come back? The queen would surely want me captured dead or alive.

At footsteps in the doorway, I glanced up to see Molly enter. With only one arm, she attempted to carry several of our buckets after standing in line with our diggings to receive food rations.

She fumbled with the containers, and at the sight of the empty sleeve where her arm should have been, a low burn flared in my gut. I'd been working at keeping the anger under control these past weeks. I'd labored as the slave of all and was doing what I could for the people while I was here. I'd thought that was enough. But what if I was capable of doing far more for them?

Curly jumped to his feet to assist Molly, taking the buckets and glancing inside to the food she'd brought us.

Why should any more people here have to lose their limbs to the rats? Or catch fevers from the fumes? Or suffer hunger because they were too exhausted to meet their daily quota?

I could feel Ty watching me. With his uncanny insight, I couldn't keep from wondering if he was able to see inside my head and read my thoughts. At the very least, he was proficient in reading my face. The other men who'd pretended to slumber during the overseer's visit had arisen and were beginning to disperse for their own evening rations, and I needed to do the same before I went through with my idea.

As Curly bent and gave Molly a tender kiss, I couldn't avert my gaze. Suddenly, all I could think about was how the two deserved to be free, to have a home of their own, a place where they could raise a dozen wee infants.

This love. These people. They were more important than anything my Testing could accomplish. I had to stop holding back and start doing whatever I could to truly help them. And if I lost my chance at being king because of it, so be it.

"Curly, I know what we must do to escape."

At my quiet statement, he backed away from Molly. From the severity of his expression, he clearly sensed the gravity of this moment.

"We must lead the slaves in an uprising tonight."

He glanced at Molly and opened his mouth as though he might protest. But at her sharp nod in my direction, he narrowed his gaze upon me.

"I know it's risky and past attempts have failed. But it's possible we may win the overseers to our plight, and then we'll only need to fight the guards."

"If we don't have weapons, we're no match."

I touched my sole. We had one knife against a dozen swords and countless arrows. Though Ty also had a knife in his boot, I refused to draw him into a battle of my making. "We have to calculate a way to steal their weapons, for our own use but also to immobilize them."

"And I suppose ye plan to be the one stealing those weapons?"

I smiled but felt no mirth. "You'd be surprised what I can accomplish with my knife."

Not only was I an expert with my seax, but I had desperation. And sometimes desperation was the mightiest weapon of all.

Chapter 14

VILMAR

I GLANCED UP AT THE TOWER GUARDHOUSE. THE CANDLELIGHT IN the upstairs room showed several guards around a table, drinking and gaming. From the open windows, they had a clear view of both barren-land and the bridge. While they were momentarily distracted with their cards and dice, they'd be at their windows the instant they heard or saw anything.

The moon overhead was a sliver in the sky, giving only faint light. So far we'd benefitted from the blackness as we worked for the past hour. In relaying the need to rescue Gabriella, Curly had gained the cooperation of several overseers. But he hadn't been able to convince them all to join us in the rebellion. Those who resisted, we'd bound and gagged.

I'd given myself the task of eliminating the two guards standing watch at the southern and western edges of Slave Town. In sneaking up behind them, I'd been so silent they hadn't heard my approach. I'd wielded my blade swiftly, jabbing into the weakest part of their armor before they could utter a sound.

In stripping them, we'd gained two swords and two daggers, along with their ill-fitting armor, which the others divided amongst themselves. Combined with the clubs and knives of the overseers as well as our mining tools and makeshift stone blades, I prayed we had enough to battle the remainder of the guards.

I eyed the dark span between the edge of town and the tower. The distance wasn't far, but it was enough that the soldiers on duty could easily notice movement there. Would I be fast and stealthy enough to remain undetected? Even if I crossed successfully, I still had to make it up inside the tower and overcome the guards.

Such a battle would give them time to alert and awaken everyone in the soldier's barracks. Additionally, if I didn't gain control of the tower, the guards would pick off every slave who attempted to cross barren-land and would also have a clear shot at anyone who stepped onto the bridge.

Our escape hinged upon me capturing the tower and the three watchmen. If I could accomplish the feat, our battle against the remaining guards would still be difficult, but possible, although we needed every slave and weapon to earn our freedom.

But we had no guarantees. I'd pleaded with Curly that if anything should happen to me, he'd leave me behind and cross over so he could usher everyone else into hiding. I also made him pledge to stop Gabriella.

With another glance up at the tower room to ensure the guards were still busy with their nightly game, I skirted the hut closest to the edge of town, took a deep breath, and then sprinted forward into barren-land, keeping my steps light and soundless, praying the darkness would conceal me.

As I raced, I kept an eye on the room. At the sight of one of the soldiers rising and crossing toward the window facing me, I scooped up a large stone and tossed it as far as I could manage toward the ravine. At the clattering, the soldier paused and veered to the other side of the tower overlooking the bridge.

His two companions pushed away from the table and joined him, their bows at the ready. I had only seconds before they rounded their post and searched barren-land as well as the town beyond. Only seconds before one of their arrows pierced me.

I pushed faster and practically threw myself the last few steps against the base of the tower. I flattened my body to the stone wall and hoped the guards wouldn't think to peer straight down, and that if they did, the shadows of the tower would conceal me.

At the soft puff of a breath beside me, I stiffened. In an instant I had my blade out and pressed against someone's throat.

"It is I." Ty's voice was barely audible.

I dropped my knife and then held myself motionless. I couldn't see the guards anymore, but from the quiet above, I knew they were still alert and searching for the cause of the clattering rock.

We didn't budge. A short while later, when the guards' voices drifted down to us, the sign they'd resumed their conversations, I allowed myself to breathe evenly. We'd escaped discovery, at least for now.

I leaned into Ty. "As I've put an end to my Testing, you're no longer obligated to protect me."

"I'm not protecting you," he whispered back. "I'm helping you set these people free."

My next admonition—for him to cease following me—stalled on my lips. After the past weeks in the mine pits and all the hardship we'd witnessed, was it possible that, like me, Ty could no longer remain passive but was compelled to fight for justice and mercy?

He ducked closer. "We will have a better chance at taking control of the tower with two of us working together."

I nodded. Especially because Ty also had a knife concealed in the sole of his boot. Though I hadn't seen him fight before, any amount of assistance would help, no matter how small. I also hoped to use the element of surprise to our advantage.

Ty and I would be outnumbered, and the tower guards would have time to sound the alarm and call for reinforcements. I had no choice but to take control of the tower if we had any chance of crossing the ravine. Hopefully, Curly and his men could hold at bay the other guards while everyone else made it across.

After long minutes elapsed and the guards began conversing again, I nudged Ty, and we rounded the tower until we reached the door. I tried the handle, but it was locked. I'd suspected it might be and thrust the tip of my knife into the keyhole, hoping to break it loose without making too much noise.

Ty pushed my hand out of the way. Before I could protest, he inserted the narrow tip of one of his quill pens. He fiddled for a few seconds before we heard the soft *click* of the lock turning. I moved to swing the door open, but he stopped me again, this time dripping some of his ink onto each of the door hinges.

Once he finished, the heavy slab moved soundlessly, and he stepped through. Surprised and grateful for his ingenuity, I followed on his heels, willing for him to take the lead, as he would need to use his ink to soften the squeal of the door at the top of the tower.

Through the dark, we climbed the steps with only the occasional squeak of a board. When we reached the landing, the light glowing from underneath the door illuminated enough of the stairwell to see that this entrance wasn't locked. Even so, Ty used his ink on the hinges.

I held my seax at the ready. When Ty pocketed his ink pot and placed a hand on the door, I halted him. I motioned to myself, indicating that I wanted to go in first.

He shook his head and pressed a thumb to his chest. Then with a sharp nod, he pushed the door. It slid open, and he slipped inside before I could jostle ahead of him. With a burst of frustration, I prayed he wouldn't get in my way or do anything to jeopardize this mission.

When I stepped in after him, he'd already crossed halfway to the closest guard before any of the three noticed he was in the room. At the sight of him, they sat up, uttered oaths, and began to scoot back from the table. But before they could stand, Ty flew at the first guard, silenced him, and was already diving for the second.

Concealing my knife, I lunged for the last one. He unsheathed his sword and swept it toward my midsection, clearly expecting to have the advantage against an unarmed slave.

With his arm upraised, I angled my knife into the weak spot of his hauberk, plunging it deeply and twisting hard before retracting it.

At the sight of my knife covered in his blood, his eyes rounded with disbelief. Then his gaze darted to his companions, both dead upon their benches and slumped on the table. He spun and fumbled for the bell rope dangling from the ceiling. Before he could touch the cord, I threw my seax, so it impaled his hand. He grabbed at the rope with his other hand, but another knife stabbed into him, this time into his neck.

With a *whoosh* that was likely his attempt at a shout, he crumpled to the floor, knocking his bench over, before lying listless.

Ty wasted no time in crossing to the man and making sure he was indeed dead. As Ty retrieved our knives, I peered out at the town, praying the other guards hadn't been awakened by the ruckus. At the ensuing silence, my pulse surged with relief.

Was it possible we would be able to leave without a major battle?

I motioned toward the town, hoping Curly would see my command and start sending everyone to the bridge. A moment later, people began to step into barren-land, cautiously at first, but then faster as no one opposed them. At a sharp whisper from someone, they slowed so the noise of footfalls in the rocks wouldn't penetrate the guardhouse.

As the first of the slaves drew near, I waved them onward to the bridge and prayed it would hold fast until the last person crossed to the other side—which I intended to be me.

Ty moved to my side and handed me my knife, wiped clean. His olive skin glistened with perspiration. He'd been small and thin before entering the mine and now was even more so. But he radiated strength as he held out a chain-mail hauberk and leather belt he'd taken from the dead. He'd already donned the gear for himself, along with a host of weapons.

"I'll hold the tower until the last person crosses," he said.

I tugged the other hauberk over my head, a veil of shame slipping over me at the same time. I'd underestimated Ty's abilities. More than that, I'd scorned my need for him and had been nothing but irritated by his hovering presence. As I let the shirt of mail fall to my thighs, I met Ty's gaze. "I owe you an apology. I have let my pride dictate my actions toward you. Instead of accepting you graciously as I ought, I have resented your presence during the Testing."

"You have been nothing but considerate, Your Highness."

"I only wish I'd realized my shortcoming earlier."

"It is not entirely your fault, Your Highness. I have done my share of holding myself back so I might remain objective."

I strapped on my belt along with the scabbard. "Let us vow to put aside the boundaries of the Testing now that I have forsaken it."

"Very well, Your Highness." He bowed his head. "Although, I should still like to record the details of our days, if Your Highness will allow it."

I didn't know what good such an account would be, and I didn't know if I wanted my father or the Lagting to read about this revolt and my part in it. But ultimately, they would need to know the reason I'd neglected to follow through with the Testing.

"If you wish, you may continue your records." I could no longer worry about disappointing my father and all the people who'd been counting on me to become the next king. "Perhaps through your accounts, everyone will come to understand—and even forgive me—for choosing to help these people over gaining the kingship."

Ty gave a slight bow before he returned to the closest soldier and divested him of the remainder of his weapons.

The slaves were now crossing the bridge. Although the repairs to the slats seemed sturdy enough and had held the transporters bringing supplies and food to town, I couldn't keep from thinking back to my first night at the camp, when the bridge had cracked, nearly sending Farthing to his death, and how Gabriella had raced out and saved his life. That had been the moment when I'd first started caring about her.

Affection for her pulsed through me, hurting me with its intensity. Heretofore, I'd wavered, hadn't wanted to allow anything to interfere with the Testing. But how could I deny my feelings any longer? My ardor had been growing every day since the first. Now it filled me so completely, I couldn't separate from it, even if I'd wanted to, which I didn't.

"Do you have a plan for how you will save her when you get to the queen's palace?" Ty asked quietly.

How had Ty known I was thinking about Gabriella? Was my passion that evident? "If I'm unable to reach her chamber, then I shall have to attend the ball."

"And while dancing, you will simply tie her up and drag her off the dance floor?"

"Yes."

"And you think the queen will allow it?"

"Let the queen or any man try to stop me."

"They may very well try once they learn of your involvement in the slave rebellion."

"I'm fully aware the queen will rise up against me. But I am prepared to suffer the consequences of my actions, including fighting without Scania's aid."

If the queen learned my true identity, I would assure her my father wasn't involved in any way with my decisions. And if I had to single-handedly fight the queen's army, I would.

"And what will these slaves do once they are free?" Ty peered out over the bridge, where people were crossing as hurriedly as they could.

Curly had assured me most of the slaves were shrewd and would find ways to disappear and avoid capture. For the weak and maimed, the task of obtaining refuge and staying safe would be much harder. Curly had suggested they go to Mercia. But I feared they wouldn't be able to flee from Warwick swiftly enough.

If only I could take them back with me to Scania. I'd give them sanctuary in my homeland. There they'd be able to build new lives for themselves as fishermen and farmers. But how could I secret the people away without the queen knowing?

I sighed as I finished strapping on the last of the weapons. "For now, the people must escape north into Inglewood Forest. Once there, Curly assures me they will be able to hide in the thick woodland and live off the forest at least until winter. I will come for them when I'm able. But if something happens to me, I want them to seek out Kresten. He'll show them compassion and come to their aid."

Inglewood Forest covered hundreds of square miles in southern Mercia as well as northern Warwick, and I didn't know how Curly and the others would be able to locate Kresten in so vast a wilderness. But I had to hold out hope that somehow, someway, our efforts to free these men and women from the mine pits wouldn't be in vain.

A short while later, as the last of the slaves began crossing, Ty and I finally descended from the tower and hurried toward the bridge. At the edge of the ravine, Curly stood guard, constantly scanning the silent town and barracks.

I handed him the extra weapons and armor we'd gained in the tower. "When we reach the bottom of the foothills, I want you to lead the frailest north to Mercia."

"Nay." He paused in donning the hauberk. "I'll be going with ye to Kensington to save Gabi."

"Molly and the others need someone to guide them."

"Molly knows the way." Curly strapped on the weapons belt over the chain mail. "Her father was once a woodcutter in the north of Warwick in the days before the queen took away licenses and forced woodcutters into the mine."

My thoughts warred within me. Curly was an honorable and good man, and I respected his desire to rescue Gabi alongside me. On the other hand, my mission was too risky. Even if I survived the fight with Grendel, the queen might still lock me—and anyone who fought with me—in her dungeons.

"Molly needs you."

"And Gabi needs all of us."

At what sounded like the banging of a door in town, I realized now wasn't the time to try to convince Curly to go with the others. Hearing the same, Curly motioned me ahead of him onto the bridge.

"Go." I squared my shoulders. "I shall take the rear."

He opened his mouth as though to argue. But at a shout from near the barracks, he spun and began to leap from slat to slat.

I pushed Ty to cross next. He resisted only an instant,

apparently seeing the determination in my face and realizing that attempting to persuade me otherwise would waste precious seconds.

I hurtled after him, and the bridge swayed dangerously with the hasty movement from all three of us. At the sudden clanging of a bell and more shouting from behind, my heart picked up pace, and I made myself go faster, closing in on Ty.

An arrow whizzed too close to my head, but I ducked and pressed onward. On the opposite side of the bridge, the others called out for us to hurry.

"Start severing the ropes," I commanded.

Several voices rose in protest.

"Now! Do it now."

Another arrow soared over my head. Thankfully, Ty and Curly were low enough that it overreached them.

At the vibration of blades against the cords holding the bridge to the posts, I lengthened my stride, skipping slats. "Go, go, go!" I called to Ty and Curly, now only a few steps away.

The bridge wobbled even more erratically as soldiers stepped onto it and chased after us. I wasn't sure how they'd been able to rally from their beds so swiftly, but I had no doubt they'd been trained for moments like this.

"Saw faster," I called to the men now that the end was in sight.

As Curly jumped from the bridge onto land, he spun and reached for Ty. At the same moment, a last frantic chop into the rope released its hold from the post. The bridge tilted. Curly held fast to Ty and dragged him the remainder of the distance to safety.

As I slipped and grabbed on to the side to keep from falling, the pressure of the knives and swords hacking into the cord ceased.

"Keep cutting!" I shouted, as the footsteps behind me drew nearer. "Sever it at once."

The vibration resumed, but only for a moment before the rope snapped. Two slats from the end, I launched myself forward, scrambling for something to grab, something to keep me from falling to my death below.

Even as I slammed into the stone edge, several pairs of hands groped for me, managing to clutch my arms and shoulders. Though the impact against the side of the ravine knocked the breath from my lungs, relief swelled inside, especially as I heard the bridge crack and fall away.

Curly and Ty and others drew me up. As I straightened, hands reached out to clasp me and pat my back. Some of the slaves wept openly with joy. Others whispered prayers of gratefulness.

Amidst the shouts and cries of the soldiers clinging to the bridge, which now dangled from the opposite side, I glanced to the moon and the stars. Dawn was only a few hours away. I had no time to waste if I wanted to reach the palace in time for the ball.

At my side and watching me with undisguised admiration, Curly seemed to be waiting for my next instructions. His men stood behind him, also waiting.

Before I could issue my next instructions, he lowered himself to one knee, and his men followed suit. "My lord." He bowed his head. "I pledge ye my fealty for as long as I have breath." His men spoke the same words, solemnly and without hesitation.

In Scania, amongst my own people, I was accustomed to such subservience. But here, at this moment, their devotion brought a swell of strange emotion to my chest. I should send them all on their way to Inglewood Forest, far away from the queen. And yet, if I denied them, I'd dishonor them.

At the very least, I must make clear my plans and the danger involved. "You know that I go to Kensington not only to save Lady Gabriella but also to destroy Grendel once and for all. If I succeed, I shall almost certainly incur the queen's wrath."

Curly stood, and the others did likewise. He braced his feet apart, unsheathed his sword, and lifted it. "Together we'll face whatever befalls us."

Gratitude swelled within me toward these brave men who could give of themselves so freely even when so much had been taken from them. I withdrew my sword, raised it, and touched it to Curly's. "May God go with us."

Chapter 15

Gabriella

The cobbled path leading up to the palace was noisy and crowded with all the maidens and their caravans arriving. My retinue of servants and knights rode close by, and we only added to the chaos. I didn't mind that we'd slowed our pace. Now that we were here, my courage and resolve seemed to have slipped away as easily as the warmth of the midsummer day.

Clouds piled up overhead, obscuring the blue sky and threatening rain. The air was laden with a damp chill that permeated the light linen cloak and hood I'd donned before leaving at daybreak. Lord Query had risen at the early hour to accompany me to the royal city. He followed closely behind me, tasked by the duchess to make sure I arrived at the palace on time.

"My lady," Sir Lucan murmured with a glance toward Lord Query. "It's not too late to turn back."

I avoided my loyal knight's gaze. Once he and the other servants had learned the true reason for my return to Rockland, their happiness had turned to sorrow. Now the pain and frustration in their eyes was too much to bear.

"I must do this, good sir." I wished I could ease the heartache of these dear servants, or at least make them understand why I had to sacrifice myself.

Sir Lucan didn't say anything more, and as we wound farther up the stone road, I shifted in my saddle so I could take in the view of the countryside. To the south, the walled city of Kensington spread out in all directions, reaching to the edges of the Foothill Plains. The fields there formed a patchwork of green and gold, the best farmland of Warwick with streams and rivers flowing out of the Gemstone Mountains, providing a natural means of irrigation.

Though I couldn't see beyond the plains to the south, I knew the land there gave way to the arid Siccum Desert, where very little could live or grow. Aside from the towns and estates built along the foothills and the once-prosperous mining communities, the rest of Warwick's industry came from the few coastal towns known for fishing.

To the north of the castle, the Gemstone Mountain range rose into a glorious array of tall peaks. I searched the gray rocky tips above the dark-green tree line until I found Ruby Mountain. It was too distant to see anything clearly, but my heart ached from missing the people I'd left behind.

They would be deep in the pits at this time of day, laboring to fill their buckets with rocks. Hopefully, not for many more days. Once the queen no longer had Grendel or the heart of the fairest maiden for her alchemy, she wouldn't be able to produce any more gems. Without jewels, she'd have no reason to send slaves into the rat-infested bowels of the earth. Of course, the queen might find an excuse for the continued killing and the utilization of the heart of the fairest maiden, but her task would be much harder to accomplish without rousing suspicion.

While I was thankful Benedict and Alice would be safe with my aunt, I wouldn't be satisfied until all my friends were delivered, including Vilmar. Though his sentence was only for a few more months, anything could happen during that time, and I feared for him. More than that, I longed for him in a way that was entirely foreign. Against my will, my thoughts strayed to him. His handsome face and light-blue eyes were emblazoned in the forefront of my mind. The softness and warmth of his kiss lingered with my every breath. And the kindness and nobility of his every action burned in my soul.

Such thoughts were futile and only made me question what I needed to do. I distracted myself by peering to the east of the city to the wide valley and the deep waters of Wraith Lake. The cliffs along the far edge sheltered Grendel somewhere deep within. On the side closest to the city, sheep and goats and cows already grazed within a central pit that had been built years ago to contain the slaughter. Opening to the shore, the grassy area was low and level, walled in with stones taken from the surrounding mountains.

In a few short hours, I'd be standing in the center of the arena waiting for Grendel to make his appearance. A shudder formed in the pit of my being and worked its way outward. At the moment it found release, a chilled wind drifted from the lake as if to confirm my fear.

I slipped my hand into the pocket of my skirt and skimmed the scabbard and smooth knife handle underneath my chemise. I'd easily located the knife that had belonged to my father. I'd hidden it in the far reaches of my wardrobe, never planning to touch it again, much less use it. But now, thanks to Vilmar's training, I wasn't afraid of it and could wield it with some proficiency. Would that skill be enough?

With a slight shake of my head, I threw off the self-doubt. I had to remain positive and keep my anxiety at bay. At the very least, my time in the mine had taught me to persevere during my darkest moments, never give up, and fight back against my fears. I would do that tonight and do it to the best of my ability.

"There she is," said someone nearby. "The queen."

The murmuring increased, and the traffic all but halted. I peered up at the grand castle that was built partly into the walls of the mountains. A regal woman and several important-looking noblemen stared down at the winding path.

From the distance, I couldn't see the queen's features entirely, but her beauty was clear both now and from times past when I'd met her. Her long ebony hair fell to her waist and glittered with jewels. In contrast to her hair, her skin was as pale as starlight. She held herself rigidly, her chin angled up and her shoulders stiff, giving off an aura of both power and majesty.

Was she examining the maidens and even now choosing which of us she'd sacrifice to the monster? After the hours of preparation, I hoped I glowed with beauty. As soon as we arrived at the palace, my servants would finish preparing me, fashioning my hair into long curls and attiring me in a shimmering emerald gown—the queen's favorite color. Ultimately, no matter what I might do or say, the choice belonged to the queen. I must be beautiful enough to catch her attention during the ball.

I studied her again from afar. If only I could get close enough to plunge my knife into her heart to put an end to her reign and avenge my father's death. I averted my gaze, and shame rushed in. My father wouldn't want me to take a life for his, not when he'd died in an attempt to put an end to violence.

As much as he'd disagreed with the queen over various policies during the years as her advisor, he'd always worked toward peaceful resolutions and advocated kindness. He'd oft quoted the Holy Scripture verse that said: *"See that none render evil for evil unto any man; but ever follow that which is good, both among yourselves, and to all men."*

I'd always carried his wisdom close to my heart. But over recent months, had I allowed my bitterness and need for revenge to cast a cloud above the need for kindness?

If he'd been alive, what would he say about my plans tonight? Would he approve?

Perhaps he'd laud me for my willingness to sacrifice myself for the greater good of all the maidens this summer and the years to come. Perhaps he'd laud me for wanting to eliminate slavery in the mine pits. Perhaps he'd even laud me for learning to wield a knife so I might defend myself against Grendel.

But in all my scheming, he wouldn't want me to shift my focus from the light of what was true and right to the darkness that could eat a soul and leave blackness in its place.

As the traffic around us began to surge forward, I nudged my mount and pushed thoughts of my father from my mind. I needed to stay focused on what I'd come to do without letting anything distract me. If that meant I had to allow in some darkness to accomplish my deed, in the end it would be worth the cost.

VILMAR

From a hidden spot on the flat roof of the livery and blacksmith, I crouched next to Curly and Ty, peering down at the inner bailey. The area teemed with horses and knights who had already delivered their maidens and were now tending to their mounts and gathering around several large fire pits for feasting.

Though cloudy, the evening sky was still bright and would be for several more hours on the longest day of the year. The daylight would make our escape with Gabriella more difficult, but I was determined to get her away from the castle and Wraith Lake as fast as I could.

"The maidens be inside already," Curly whispered.

I fought back my frustration that we'd arrived too late to intercept her before she entered the castle. Curly had described the chaos and confusion that ensued while the caravans of women were climbing the hill to reach the palace, and we'd hoped to wind through the crowds, mingle with the masses, reach Gabriella, and sneak her away with no one the wiser for her disappearance.

However, as Curly had led the dozen or so of us men

through the backcountry trails, we happened upon a hunting party and needed to hide until they passed. Though we ran the last miles and pushed ourselves to the brink of exhaustion, we missed our opportunity to snatch Gabriella.

The others who'd accompanied us now waited by Wraith Lake. I'd wanted Ty to stay with them, but he'd insisted on remaining by my side. This time, only gratefulness welled up for this faithful servant who had nothing to gain in my venture and wanted to help nonetheless.

With time slipping away, I needed to act soon to ensure I had enough time not only to hide her, but also to return and offer to battle Grendel. Curly had assured me that, if I stepped forward and presented myself as a contender to fight the berserker, the queen would allow it. Others had done so over the years, especially fathers and sons who'd hoped to eliminate Grendel and in so doing protect their daughters and sisters.

None had ever succeeded, and the queen would assume I would fail as well. But with my background, I would hopefully have an advantage. Not only had I received weapons training from the best warriors in Scania, but I'd also watched the best knights in my country battle against the berserkers. Though I'd been but a boy at the time, I still remembered the techniques they used to lure and trap the madmen.

Besides, my companions would be nearby and, at my signal, would come to my aid. Together, we would defeat Grendel.

"I shall go in and get her." I started to rise.

Curly yanked me down. "Ye cannot just walk in the main door. The queen has extra guards stationed throughout the palace for keeping away desperate families and lovers."

Apparently, I wasn't the first person to try to rescue one of the women, but I hoped I'd be the last. Once I killed Grendel, no other maiden would have to suffer this custom ever again.

"I must go in," I insisted.

Curly was silent for a moment, his keen gaze studying the palace. "They'll be starting the dance erelong. Maybe ye can creep inside and pull her away then."

My mind whirled with the possibility. How would I be able to haul her off without everyone seeing me? Especially with the grime of the mines filling every crevice. "I shall need to bathe and don the appropriate attire."

Both Curly and Ty lifted their brows.

"I'll attend the dance as a guest. As I'm twirling with Gabriella, I'll guide us toward the side of the room, to a secluded area. Once there, we'll sneak off."

Curly nodded, his red hair wild and untamed in the dampness that permeated the summer air. "That might work. I know a place by the buttery that leads down to a cellar entrance. Ty and I can wait for ye there."

"But transforming the master?" Ty gave me a once-over that told me I looked as bad as I smelled.

Curly assessed me as well. "Aye, ye be needing some work if ye hope to pass for a nobleman."

"Can you aid me?"

"I can be getting ye clothing and hot water. Beyond that, I'm no good."

"If you find those items," Ty whispered, "I'll take care of the rest."

An hour later, I was ready for the ball. Curly had

located garments in the servants' quarters amongst the mending pile. Though the tunic needed a few stitches to close up a gaping hole under one arm and the hose required the patching of a rip in the backside, Ty had worked magic not only on the clothing but on me. In an abandoned part of the cellar devoid of servants, he helped me scrub two months of filth from my body, washed and trimmed my hair, and helped me shave.

By the time I hovered on the outer edges of the milling crowds in the grand hall, I blended in so well no one glanced my way. The atmosphere was decidedly quieter and more somber than any ball I'd ever attended, even with the cheerful music the minstrels were playing on their flutes, fiddles, and lutes.

No one was yet dancing, and I scanned the crowd for Gabriella, hoping to identify her by her red hair. At the pause of the music and the silence descending over the gathering, I shifted my attention to the double grand staircases made of gleaming marble and the rounded balcony connecting them.

In the center and poised above the hall, the queen stood, elegant in a gown with layers of gauzy green and bedecked with spotless ermine. Her dark hair hung in long waves and glittered with what appeared to be dozens of pearls and diamonds. The crown resting on her head also gleamed with hundreds of iridescent jewels.

For a queen in her midlife, she had retained a youthfulness and beauty that would have made her a contender for the fairest maiden if such a thing had existed when she'd been younger. Although elegant, her bearing contained too much haughtiness for my liking.

At the commotion around me, I realized the lords and ladies had lowered themselves to their knees and bowed their heads, and now I was the only one standing. Something inside me resisted having to bow to this queen. She wasn't my ruler. I didn't owe her my allegiance. And I most certainly didn't respect her, not after everything I'd learned about her.

But I forced myself down to the ground. I needed to blend in better and exert more caution until Gabriella was safe. After several more long moments of silence, the queen spoke. "Let the presentation of the fairest maidens in the land begin."

As I rose with the others, I realized the queen was staring directly at me, her green eyes cold and yet inscrutable. My failure to immediately bow had garnered notice. Or perhaps she was curious because I didn't cower before her like everyone else.

Using the self-control I'd developed during my time in the mine, I pushed down my rights along with my pride. I dropped my gaze and bowed my head, attempting to show her the subservience she commanded of her people.

When the music began again, this time softer and more melodic, I glanced up to see that the maidens had started their procession. Thankfully, the queen's attention was diverted from me. From each of the staircases, the women descended, pausing briefly on each step as though to give the queen plenty of time to assess them. Attired in vibrant green gowns and with flowing hair, the sight of so many beautiful women would have been breath-taking, except I could only picture the brutality awaiting one of them in a few short hours.

At the image of blood darkening the green, anger sliced through me. How could the queen perpetuate this sickening ritual year after year, not only putting the women and their families through this choosing process,

171

but then subjugating a helpless maiden to Grendel's slaughter? How dare she? And for what gain? So she could have more wealth for herself? More jewels for her hair and gowns?

My fingers found the hilt of the stolen sword at my hip, and I gripped it tightly. I understood more clearly why Gabriella wanted to kill Grendel, why she'd been willing to sacrifice herself if need be.

At that moment, Gabriella arrived at the top of the grand staircase to my left, the last of the two dozen women. The layers of her fluttering emerald gown served to highlight the paleness of her skin and the golden red of her hair that swirled in long, wavy curls. Her features glowed with an almost ethereal beauty, more so than I remembered.

My heartbeat raced forward into a thundering gallop, first in awe of her beauty, but then in dread. She was easily the fairest woman present. And tonight of all nights, beauty was a curse.

As she started down the steps, pausing at each one, I had to hold myself back from running to her, sweeping her up, and carrying her off. *Patience.* If I had any hope of stealing her away, I had to have patience. Even then, my task would be more difficult, since the queen would likely be watching Gabriella the closest.

My frustration mounted when the dancing started and guards took their places at every doorway in the room—including the buttery. I stayed in the shadows of the grand hall for the first few dances, studying the entries and the open windows, trying to determine how to accomplish the rescue. But the longer I attempted to map a new route, the more discouraged I grew.

We were trapped. Would I have to fight our way out?

Finally, as the music of a dance came to an end, I strode out into the room, heading for Gabriella. One young man stood with her, a sad smile upon his face. He likely knew as well as everyone else that Gabriella would be chosen, and he'd probably danced with her out of pity.

When I was only steps away, Gabriella glanced up, saying something to her partner but then halting as she caught sight of me. Her beautiful blue eyes widened and filled with both wonder and surprise.

Her lips rounded as if to question my presence there, but I quickly cut her off. "May I have this next dance, my lady?" I couldn't chance her questioning me about the mine pits and how I happened to escape.

I wasn't yet sure if news of the revolt had reached the capital city. But it would erelong, if it hadn't already. When the word spread, I had no wish for anyone to implicate me—at least, not until I had the chance to save Gabriella and kill Grendel.

Before Gabriella could accept my offer, I reached for her hand, clasped it with mine, and then fitted my other hand at her waist. As if on cue, the music began again, and I moved in the steps of the dance. Though I liked the lively traditional dancing of Scania better, Mother had introduced the more elegant dances of the Great Isle into court, giving me no choice but to learn them.

Now as I led Gabriella, I was thankful to my mother for imparting her customs that allowed me to fit in to the gathering.

"What are you doing here?" she whispered, staring up at me, still wide-eyed. "How did you get away—?"

I quickly bent in and brushed my lips across hers, hoping to muffle her words from anyone dancing near us. I hadn't planned on kissing her, hadn't even thought about what I was doing until my lips meshed with hers.

She responded immediately, almost eagerly. And though everything within me longed to press in and keep on kissing her, I broke away and shifted my mouth to her ear. For several heartbeats, I couldn't speak, too overcome by her nearness. Finally, I managed a whisper. "Don't say anything about the mine."

She nodded imperceptibly.

As I pulled back again to a proper distance, I glanced around to see who might have observed our interaction. The queen, still standing on the balcony above the dance floor, seemed occupied in conversing with two men with tonsured hair rings and long brown habits. I guessed they were monks, perhaps the priests who helped the queen decide which of the maidens would best meet the qualification for her alchemy ingredient?

When I returned my attention to Gabriella, I caught her gazing up at me—at my mouth—with such longing I had to close my eyes and fight the urge to kiss her again, this time thoroughly.

I took a deep breath. I wasn't here to indulge my passions. I'd come to save her life, and that meant I couldn't afford to make a single mistake.

"I cannot believe you are here," she whispered. "I feel as though I am in a dream, and I have no wish to wake up from it."

I opened my eyes to find she was smiling a small, gentle smile. Up close, I could see that her skin was perfect, her features flawless, and her hair gleaming. Yes, she'd been pretty, even in her ragged condition in the mines. But here, now, she was a vision of radiance. This was the way she was meant to be, the way she ought to be from this day forward.

"You look too good to be true." This time she examined me more openly.

"Ty did his best to make me presentable."

"He made you incredibly handsome." The moment the words left her lips, she blushed, and her lashes fell, hiding her eyes.

"It was no easy task." I tried to keep my tone light to put her at ease.

"'Twas likely no trouble, since you are already so good-looking." Her cheeks flamed brighter. "I love your eyes most of all."

As our gazes collided, I wanted to revel in her praise, but I suspected her tongue was loose because she believed her end was near. The imminence of death oft had a way of breaking down reserves and making one say things otherwise hidden.

"Now that you are here, I shall dance with no other." She slid her free hand over my heart and held it there.

Something in the depths of her eyes told me she cared as deeply about me as I did her. Dare I express myself? What did I have to lose? If her tongue could be so loosened, then why not allow mine to be just as loose? "I want no one else but you, Gabriella."

Her long lashes fanned up, making her even more beautiful. "And I want no one but you."

I didn't care if she'd responded in kind because she didn't believe we would have any tomorrows left. Regardless, I let her words flow through me, sparking a new plan and giving me the fortitude to do what I knew I must. Though I might not be able to find a way to take her out of the castle, I might be able to stand in her place and sacrifice myself in her stead.

Chapter 16

Gabriella

Vilmar was here, and he wanted me. I tried not to think about how his impassioned words could lead nowhere and that we had no future. Instead I focused on tonight, these dances, this closeness. I would cherish every single second together until the end.

I didn't care that I was staring at him and memorizing each of his ruggedly handsome features. I didn't care that I'd gushed over him and revealed how much I adored him. I simply wanted to stay in the circle of his arms, with my hand resting against his heart, feeling his strong and steady lifeblood and letting it lend me his strength.

Yes, I was curious how he'd escaped the mine. Somehow he must have been able to arrange an early release. Had he come here specifically to see me? Had he figured out my plans?

Though the questions swirled within me, I refrained from asking them. I didn't want to waste any of our last minutes together worrying. He was safe, and that was what mattered.

As we danced, the sun set, and servants lit more candles throughout the grand hall. After several dances, he leaned closer, pressed his face into my hair, and drew in a deep breath. "When I came to Warwick, I never planned to get involved like this, but I did."

Came to Warwick? What did he mean?

"You changed everything," he whispered before I could voice my query. "And no matter what happens, I know I'm doing the right thing."

My heart lurched with misgiving. "Whatever do you mean?" I pulled back slightly to read his expression.

He didn't meet my gaze and instead turned his attention to the balcony. "When you leave here tonight, I want you to go with Ty. He'll take you away from Warwick back to my homeland. There you will never have to worry again."

My feet stalled. I was thoroughly confused. If he wasn't from Warwick, then why had he been sentenced to work in the mine?

He stopped dancing too, his focus on the queen.

I cupped his chin and gently turned his head back to me. The blue of his eyes was icy, frozen with determination. "Where is your homeland?"

He hesitated.

"Please tell me."

"Scania."

"Then why are you here in Warwick?"

"Ty will explain it to you later."

"I cannot go with Ty." I stroked his cheek. Though he'd shaven, a slight layer of stubble remained and was rough beneath my fingers. How could I explain my mission tonight? That I might not survive? "Remember the enemy I told you I must kill?"

His eyes narrowed. "I've already discovered your true intentions, Gabriella. And that's why I'm here tonight. I won't let you fight Grendel."

I should have known that by departing from the mine so close to Midsummer's Eve, he would easily add up everything I'd told him. What I couldn't have anticipated was that he'd leave and try to stop me. How had he managed to get out?

No matter how he'd done it, he wouldn't be able to make me change my mind. "Someone must fight. And I would that it be me and not one of the other young maidens."

"It shall be none of you, ever again," he whispered fiercely. With that, he released me. Before I could grab him back, he was maneuvering away from me through the swirling nobility, and I lost sight of him.

I stood on my toes, searching frantically, a terrible premonition rising within me. He was planning to do something, and I dreaded what that might be.

"Your Majesty." His voice boomed above the music and conversation.

As the other dancers slowed to stillness, I glimpsed him at the bottom of the queen's balcony, his handsome head held high and his broad shoulders straight.

What was he doing addressing the queen? My pulse picked up pace, a warning thrumming through my blood, a warning that his interaction with the queen would only end badly.

As silence descended over the grand hall, the queen, in quiet conversation with the priests who stood on either side of her, paused and glanced down at Vilmar. Irritation flickered across her features, the kind that said she'd hoped to avoid such a scene tonight and was frustrated she must now confront a protestor.

Invariably, such confrontations happened every year. We heard about them after the ball, the rumors regarding one family member or another who experienced a breakdown or went mad. The queen almost always locked such protestors away in the dungeons until after the sacrifice.

Such madness was to be expected from the people who had to forfeit their loved ones in so brutal a custom. Even so, I couldn't let Vilmar say anything. I pushed through the crowd, desperate to stop him before he put himself at risk.

"Your Majesty," he said again, his tone filling with authority. "I am Prince Vilmar, son of King Christian of the Holberg kings from the great kingdom of Scania."

Gasps and murmurs rose into the air around me. But the surprise of the other guests couldn't compare to my own. My feet slowed to a halt, and every function within my body seemed to cease.

Vilmar was a prince?

I shook my head, trying to deny his words. He'd been a slave in the mine pits. And he'd labored next to the rest of us without any privileges, facing the same dangers and experiencing the same deprivations. How could he be a prince? Was he merely saying so? And for what purpose?

The irritation fled from the queen's pale face, replaced instead by curiosity. "Prince Vilmar? You are the second son of King Christian?"

"Yes, Your Majesty."

The queen regarded Vilmar for a long silent moment. "And how does my father's sister, Queen Joanna fare?"

"She fares well."

Not only was Vilmar a prince, but he was a cousin to Queen Margery? I scrambled to recall the history of the Great Isle. If I remembered correctly, King Alfred the Peacemaker had secured an alliance with Scania through the marriage of his youngest sister, Joanna. In doing so, he'd put an end to the warring raids of the Scanian people and brought about peace.

The queen continued to scrutinize Vilmar. "You are rumored to be next in line for the kingship."

Vilmar bowed his head in acknowledgment of the queen's statement.

My heartbeat pounded harder. I couldn't begin to make sense of anything the queen and Vilmar were saying. Certainly Vilmar wasn't in line to become king of one of the Great Isle's strongest allies. How could he be? He wasn't royalty. No prince would ever be subjected to the degradation and danger of the mine.

"I'm here in Warwick for my Testing." His voice rang with a disconcerting authority I hadn't heard there before.

What was this Testing? I wanted to push my way to the forefront of the crowd and demand that Vilmar explain himself, tell me the truth about who he was and his purpose in Warwick. If he truly was a prince as he claimed, then he'd been lying to me all these weeks.

"Ah yes, the Testing," the queen replied. "So Scania still insists on its barbaric and antiquated way of determining its king?"

"It cannot be as barbaric as your yearly custom of sacrificing a maiden to Grendel." Vilmar's accusation was met with stony silence.

His words from moments ago came back to me, his response to my desire to fight Grendel so none of the other women would have to: *It shall be none of you, ever again.*

Suddenly I began to tremble. What was he planning?

"As you know," he continued, "Grendel is one of the berserkers who used to inhabit the land of Scania. When my father waged war to capture the madmen, Grendel escaped from his knights and came to dwell here."

"Yes," the queen replied. "'Tis the story I am told."

"Then you will conclude, as I have, that my family is partly to blame for Grendel's reign of terror in your land."

"Your family is mostly to blame."

Of course the queen would agree. Then she needn't accept responsibility for perpetuating the sacrifices over the years.

Vilmar bowed his head once more, clearly accepting the blame, although he knew from all I'd told him of the queen's true reason for allowing the sacrifices to continue.

"Since we are in agreement," Vilmar continued, "then you would do my family and country a great honor by allowing me the chance to slay the beast."

A cry of protest rose swiftly within me, and I started forward again, fraught with the need to end Vilmar's conversation with the queen. And yet, even as I stumbled closer, my chest ached with an undeniable truth.

I must allow Vilmar to face Grendel.

He had a better chance of slaying the monster and bringing an end to the queen's alchemy ritual than I did. How could I oppose his offer when it could save many lives in the years to come?

I pressed my fist against my mouth to stifle the objection. Anything I might say would only stem from selfish motives—primarily because I cared for Vilmar and didn't want to see him confront so great a danger. But also because all along, I'd wanted to get even with the queen and seek revenge for my father's death.

The queen was silent for a moment, then shook her head. "You are noble to request to atone for King Christian's mistakes. But over the years, many strong warriors and great knights have attempted to slay Grendel, and no one has prevailed."

"Their failures are of no consequence to me."

"Yes, but your failure and subsequent death will have consequences for me, quite possibly angering Scania at the loss of so valuable a prince."

I suspected the queen didn't truly care if she angered Scania. She was merely attempting to sway Vilmar away from his quest so she need not fear losing Grendel.

"Your Majesty, let these noble people here in your grand hall be our witnesses. If I must sacrifice my life in an attempt to end Grendel's, then all will know I did so freely. Thus, you and your kingdom will not be held responsible for my death."

As the excited whispers and murmurs increased around the room, the queen would be left with no choice but to allow Vilmar the opportunity to fight Grendel. The people were looking for a hero, someone to rescue them from the monster. She couldn't deny them this chance, not without making herself look calloused and unconcerned.

As if coming to the same conclusion, the queen bowed her head to Vilmar. "My guests here tonight shall be our witnesses."

"If I lose, my country cannot take revenge. So long as you grant me one wish . . ."

The queen lifted her head and met Vilmar's gaze levelly. Her eyes were cold and would have made any other person shiver in fear. "And what wish is that, Your Highness?"

"You will allow me to choose a bride from amongst these fair maidens and marry her before going to fight."

At his declaration, my breath caught in my lungs. A bride? Did he mean me? But how could he? I was no longer a wealthy heiress with a substantial dowry. Even if I regained my riches from the duchess—which was doubtful—I didn't belong to a family of importance who could provide a political alliance for Scania. In fact, I was a nobody with nothing. Surely his country would disapprove of him taking me as a bride.

"If you live," the queen said contemptuously, "you will be made king and will have a royal bride chosen for you."

"By agreeing to fight the berserker, I earn the right to choose my own bride."

She paused for several heartbeats. "The law in our country states a maiden must reach the age of twenty before being allowed to marry. Therefore, you cannot marry any woman present tonight, not until she reaches the legal age."

"Very well. Then we shall become betrothed."

The queen opened her mouth as if to argue with Vilmar further. Then she shrugged. "If that is what you wish, who am I to convince you otherwise?"

"Then let all the people here testify to our agreement."

"Very well."

Vilmar's instructions from earlier—especially those having to do with Ty taking me to Scania—made more sense in light of the revelation that he was a prince. Whether he won or lost the battle with Grendel, he wanted to offer me a safe future, and what better way than to become married or betrothed? Perhaps he was worried the queen would never allow me to have my freedom, not if there was a chance I could reveal the secret ingredient of her alchemy.

But the queen didn't know my father had told me the secret, did she?

As if I'd spoken aloud, the queen's attention shifted to me and her eyes narrowed. "Prince Vilmar, you have danced with only one maiden this night. Is Lady Haleigh your choice of a bride?"

The crowds around me parted, and all eyes came to rest upon me, including Vilmar's. Gone was the tenderness and affection from moments ago. Instead, his expression was as regal and haughty as the queen's. "Yes, she is the one."

"Step forward, Lady Haleigh." The queen beckoned me with one of her bejeweled hands. "We shall have the betrothal ceremony this very instant before the hour grows too late."

My objection rose but lodged in my throat. I didn't want to agree to Vilmar's plans, but if this was what I must do to destroy Grendel and the queen's yearly sacrifice, then I must endeavor to stay strong.

As one of the queen's priests made his way down the staircase, I approached Vilmar, my steps hesitant. I thought I'd known this handsome man, but he'd withheld so much of who he really was from me. What else hadn't he told me?

But even as I battled mistrust, my own deception unveiled before me. I was hypocritical. I'd been less than honest with him about my intention to fight Grendel. How could I condemn him for not saying anything to me about being a prince when I'd withheld so much? If he was participating in some kind of testing to determine his worthiness in becoming the next king, perhaps he'd been bound to secrecy regarding his identity.

As I took my place next to Vilmar, he held himself rigidly and stared straight ahead. I did likewise, already missing the closeness and sweetness we'd shared when we danced. The queen remained at the balcony, while the priest took his place in front of us. He uttered a short prayer, read a Scripture verse, and then joined our right hands.

With Vilmar's fingers holding mine, I wanted to believe this was somehow real, that he loved me enough to promise me forever. But the reality was, he'd brought up marriage as a means of rescuing me from a dire predicament. Nothing more. After all, hadn't he told me back at the mine that he was in no position to make promises to any woman, no matter how much he'd grown to care about her?

Vilmar repeated his vow after the priest. "In the name of our Lord, I, Prince Vilmar, promise that I will one day take thee as my wife, according to the ordinances of God and the holy church."

I repeated my vow, and then the priest placed the cross from his necklace on top of our hands and bound them together with the leather string. "We here bear witness to thy solemn proposal, and I declare thee betrothed. In the name of the Father, and of the Son, and of the Holy Ghost. Amen."

The priest unwrapped the strap, stood back, and made the sign of the cross. "You may seal your vow with a kiss."

Vilmar shifted slightly, hesitantly. I guessed he was having second thoughts about this betrothal. It was legally binding and could not be broken except for an annulment. If he survived the terrible fight ahead, I would grant him the annulment. I wanted him to know that, but I could not say that now.

Instead, I lifted my face, giving him access to the required kiss.

His gaze landed full upon my lips, and his pupils darkened with wanting. As he bent his head, I tingled with anticipation, though I knew I shouldn't. Nevertheless, as he pressed into me, I gave way to the pleasure of his warmth and the fervency of his mouth against mine. The fusing lasted but a few seconds before he tore himself away.

I longed to gather him back and kiss him again. But with so many people watching us and with the strike of the midnight hour drawing ever nearer, I would have to be satisfied with the brief touch.

His fingers lingered against mine, and for an eternal, blissful second his beautiful eyes filled with something I could only describe as love. As quickly as it appeared, it was gone, replaced by a rigid wall. He released my hand and gave a curt nod, which I sensed was his farewell.

Chapter 17

VILMAR

I WAS READY TO BATTLE THE BERSERKER. NOW THAT I'D SECURED Gabriella's future, I could rest in the knowledge that if anything happened to me this night, she was my betrothed. The queen couldn't touch her, and she'd find security in going to Scania. My family would take her in and provide for her out of loyalty to me. At least, I hoped they would.

My father and the Lagting would be disappointed in my rash decision to bind myself to Gabriella. Especially after they'd already begun negotiations with other countries in securing brides for each of us princes. But since I hadn't been able to find a way to sneak her out of the grand hall, my pledge was the only way I could protect her.

The memory of her lips—the soft pressure of her response, eager and with an edge of passion—beckoned me to return and explore. But I pulled myself up and took another step away, not daring to look at her again, lest I find myself unable to stop from kissing her again.

Yearning for her would only make the fight against Grendel all the more distracting and difficult. I would fare better entering the battle focused on what I must do and not on what I might lose.

"Since the hour draws nigh to Midsummer's Eve," the queen's brittle voice commanded attention, "we have our champion who will fight against Grendel, and we are grateful for his willingness to try to make up for the sins of his father before him."

The silence was broken by excited chattering and clapping.

I bowed my head to the queen, unwilling to meet her gaze lest she see my contempt. If my father had once been able to capture and subdue all the other berserkers, surely the queen could have contained this one. But I would not say so, not at this moment. I couldn't jeopardize my precarious status. If she realized I was aware of her secret, she would make certain I died one way or another.

"Prince Vilmar shall be fitted with the best armor and best weapons Warwick has to offer," the queen declared.

This time her announcement was met with cheering.

"My knights will escort you to the weapons room, where you will have access to the arms of your choosing." She nodded toward one of the guards standing in the main doorway.

"Thank you, Your Majesty." I started toward the door.

"In the meantime," her voice trailed me, "we shall proceed with our Choosing Ceremony."

My steps faltered, and I halted. The crowd grew silent, tension returning to the room and my body. Stiffly, I faced the queen once more. "There is no need for the choosing tonight, as I will slay the beast."

Her lips curved into a slight smile, one that seemed to mock me. "I was abundantly clear that no one has ever fought Grendel and lived to tell about it."

"Tonight I shall do just that."

"You are quite confident, Your Highness." Her smile crept higher. "But I am sure all my subjects will agree that we cannot take any chances. If you fail and we have not provided Grendel with a maiden, he will continue his rage throughout the land and kill countless innocent people this night."

A foreboding chill slithered through my body like a serpent waiting to strike.

Likely seeing the chill upon my features, the queen waved a hand as though to dismiss me. "You need not worry, my dear cousin. I shall honor your betrothal to Lady Haleigh, and she will be exempt from the choosing—"

"No," Gabriella said from where she still stood underneath the balcony. "If a maiden must still be sacrificed to Grendel, then I offer myself."

"Gabriella, no," I said harshly. "You will not do this."

"This is why I came—"

"No, I cannot allow it."

Her gaze reached across the distance between us and pierced me. The plea in her eyes and the sorrow there told me this was what she'd been preparing for all along. "If a maiden must go tonight to face Grendel, then I would it be me."

I could feel the queen watching our interaction. Had she anticipated this? Was that why she protested so little to our betrothal? Perhaps she'd learned of our connection in the mine pits. If she hadn't yet, she'd soon figure out why we were familiar with one another. And once learning of my part in the slave revolt, she'd make sure I never left her country. Now that she'd garnered my promise in front of witnesses that Scania couldn't hold Warwick responsible for my death, she'd discover some way to kill me and make it appear like an accident.

All the more reason I had to ensure that Gabriella left Warwick immediately. If she remained here alive, I had no doubt Queen Margery would use her to control me, for there was nothing I would not do for Gabriella, and the queen had certainly gleaned that by now.

"You must go," I said more adamantly.

"Then you would have one of these other maidens face Grendel?" Gabriella glanced over the other young women standing amongst the crowd, their beauty and emerald gowns setting them apart from everyone else, along with the fear that had now returned to each of their faces.

One of the fair maidens sidled closer to her dance partner, a gray-haired man that must be her father. He wrapped his arm around her and kissed the top of her head, his eyes bright with unshed tears.

How could I stand by and allow any of these women to face Grendel? I couldn't. And yet, what alternative did I have? If not Gabriella, the queen would select another. After the weeks of training, at least Gabriella would have some knowledge of how to defend herself.

Was this, then, our only choice? That we sacrifice our lives to Grendel together?

Gabriella nodded. She must have seen my capitulation in the droop of my shoulders.

"Your Highness." She lowered herself to one knee, bowing before the queen. "According to the custom of the Midsummer's Eve ball, I offer myself as a willing sacrifice this night."

I'd learned enough about the ceremony to know that if a maiden offered herself voluntarily, the queen and her priests must still decide. Of course, they could only use the heart of the fairest maiden in their alchemy. Was it wrong of me to pray that they would determine one of the other women was more beautiful than Gabriella?

But even as I fought for some glimmer of hope, the queen extended her scepter. "I accept your offer." Her voice rang over the assembly. "And on behalf of the people of Warwick, I thank you for your willingness to sacrifice one life for many."

Gabriella bent her head so her copper tresses fell and covered her face. Even in her state of subservience, she was exquisitely beautiful, so much so that a mingling of helplessness and rage gripped my heart. I could do nothing but spin and stalk out of the grand hall.

An hour later, attired in full armor, I stood on the cliff overlooking Wraith Lake and the grassy pit below that was to be my battleground. It was not lost on me that, in leaving the mine, I'd exchanged one pit for another.

Though I'd donned armor from the queen's weapon room and equipped myself from amongst the offerings there, I kept my seax at the front of my belt, along with the sword my father had given me on the day of commissioning for the Testing. I'd left the special weapon with Lord Kennard upon our arrival in Warwick, and somehow Ty had managed to get him word of my predicament. He'd only just arrived in the capital city, breathless and worried, pleading with me to reconsider my course of action.

"I've been present at the sacrifice before." He spoke gravely beside me, staring out over the walled area below. "And to this day, I have nightmares of the monster and his bloodthirsty massacre."

"I thank you for your concern, my lord. But I've already made up my mind to face Grendel, and nothing can convince me otherwise." Especially now that Gabriella would be there. I was left with no choice but to kill him before he reached her.

"This sacrifice exceeds the bounds of your Testing." He was familiar with our Testing, since he'd lived in Scania during the years he'd been Warwick's ambassador.

"I have given up the Testing."

At the finality of my statement, Lord Kennard fell silent, his heavy breathing filling the night air along with the calls from the guards now stationing themselves around the upper perimeter of the pit. I searched for Gabriella but could not find her yet amongst those who'd gathered.

The crowd was small, encompassing only those who'd attended the ball. I'd learned the queen required them to also watch the sacrifice, heaping upon them only more trauma.

The rest of the citizens of Warwick were hiding behind closed doors, no doubt praying Grendel would be satisfied with this sacrifice, so he didn't break free of the pit and seek more death and destruction.

The guards began to light the torches in the cliff walls, illuminating the arena. Already I could make out the forms of the livestock, resting peacefully in the grass, heedless of the brutality to be unleashed upon them erelong.

I could only pray the torchlight wouldn't reveal the boat where Ty, Curly, and the others waited, ready to lend me aid when I signaled for them.

"You may have given up the Testing," Lord Kennard finally said, "but the Testing has not given up you."

"I have no time for riddles, my lord. I give you leave to speak freely."

The stately man clasped my shoulder the way my father might have had he been here. The pressure was kindly, even against my armor. "The engraving on your sword." He nodded toward my belt.

Be slave of all. I skimmed my fingers over the words before I sheathed the weapon.

"During my ride to Kensington," Lord Kennard said, "I have been pondering the message behind the engraving."

"Then you are not alone in your musings, for I have sought to know the true meaning of my challenge since the first day."

"I cannot lay claim to knowing the *true meaning* as you call it. But I could not keep from thinking of the Scripture verses connected to the words of your engraving. They are found in the Gospel of Mark and say something like: The Lord did not come to be served, but to serve, and to lay down his life as a ransom for many."

Since leaving Scania, I'd had no access to the rare holy verses and hadn't been able to put my challenge into the context of Scripture. I shouldn't have been surprised to find so strong an admonition, but I was nonetheless.

"While I cannot condone what you are doing here tonight," Lord Kennard continued, "I believe you are following in Christ's footsteps in being willing to serve, even unto death itself. In doing so, you are fulfilling your Testing."

"I'm battling Grendel for myself, not for the Testing." I glanced around, making sure none of the queen's men were nearby to hear my confession. "As I said, I have given the Testing up. Even if I should live past tonight, I cannot go back to being a slave in the mines."

He observed my face, then lowered his voice. "Then the rumors regarding the slave revolt are true?"

I nodded.

"You were noble to attempt to end the slavery. But as long as gems lie in the depths of the mountains, the queen will enslave the people."

All the more reason why I needed to kill Grendel tonight and put an end to the queen's alchemy. If I didn't save Gabriella's life, her heart would be the next used in making the jewels grow in the mine pits. I couldn't fathom having even a piece of her return to the dark passageways. The very idea made me sick to my stomach.

More torches glowed around the tall stone walls, shining down onto the pastureland below. I wasn't sure if I should be glad for the full lighting that would allow me to see my enemy's every move or appalled that the gruesome battle must be displayed so spectacularly.

As I studied the grassy area and attempted to gain a familiarity with the setting, my gaze snagged on a stone table at the center. Upon it stood a beautiful woman, her long hair rippling in the breeze along with her emerald gown.

Even from a distance, I had no trouble recognizing Gabriella or the chains linked around each of her feet, binding her to the altar with no way to escape.

Panic surged into my veins. Though I wasn't surprised by her presence in the pit, I was surprised by the intensity of my reaction. I loathed the prospect of her being anywhere near the berserker. Loathed the queen for her greed and cruelty. And loathed myself for not rescuing her the way I'd intended.

Once Grendel arrived, I could not fail her again.

Chapter
18

Gabriella

I stared out over the gently rolling waves of Wraith Lake, waiting for my first glimpse of Grendel rowing toward the shore.

I tried to still my shaking, especially in my hands. If I didn't, I wouldn't be able to plunge my knife into the primary artery in Grendel's neck. I needed to remain calm and steady, since I'd likely only get one chance to stab him before he sliced into me.

At a distant howl, my skin crawled. Was that Grendel leaving his cave dwelling?

I glanced to the sky overhead to gauge the passing of time, but the cloud cover remained thick, showing neither moon nor stars. However, the torches above had been lit, the flames throwing off flickering shadows that danced in merriment around me, as if the wraiths had come out of the depths of the mountain to celebrate my sacrifice.

My thoughts returned to Vilmar's stricken face when I'd offered myself as the fairest maiden. He'd wanted so badly to save me from facing Grendel that he'd pledged me his troth even though doing so would bring censure from his family, especially if he was next in line to be king of Scania.

By volunteering to be the chosen one, I'd ruined his well-intentioned plans. But I prayed he understood I couldn't run away from Grendel and Warwick. If I left and tried to ignore the problems, they'd haunt me the rest of my life. I'd never have peace because I would always regret not confronting the evil when I'd had the opportunity.

Another howl filled the air, this time closer. Grendel. He was on his way.

The people on the cliffs above grew silent. In their elevated positions, they could see farther than I could. But even with their view, they'd take no joy in watching Grendel come ashore and destroy everything and everyone in his path. They would be horribly saddened and sickened by all they witnessed, just as I'd been during the one year the queen had ordered all of her advisors and their families to attend.

I shifted, the manacles around my ankles tight and digging into my skin. The short length of chain holding me in place clinked. I wouldn't be able to run away from Grendel when he charged toward me. I would hardly be able to move to protect myself.

Of course, the queen defended her use of the chains, claiming that she was keeping Grendel from taking the maiden's body. Every year after the slaughter, he loaded his boat with the livestock he'd killed until the hull sank low in the water. Some speculated he dried the meat and subsisted on it during the winter months. Others said he ate all the meat in one great feast.

Whatever the case, he'd never been able to carry away the maiden's body. The queen made sure of it, and I was one of the few who knew the real reason why.

On a high cliff to the north of the arena, the queen stepped down and sat upon one of her jeweled thrones, which had been placed there for the occasion. She settled in and sipped from a goblet, almost as if she were attending a dinner party rather than a massacre.

The growls and grunts became louder, echoing and sending chills down my spine. The madman was drawing nearer. How long before his boat appeared in the torchlight that touched upon the black water just off the shore? Likely only minutes.

I pinched my eyes closed and tried to draw in a deep breath. "This is for you, Father. To avenge your death." But the words seemed to suck the life from me rather than give me the energy I desired.

"And this is for all the slaves who have ever died or been maimed in the mine pits." I'd hoped the declaration would give me a surge of strength, but only emptiness remained.

I had to kill or be killed. That was the way to survive this night. Wasn't it?

A roaring scream resounded off the cliffs and bounced against me, and I couldn't contain a shudder. The outline of a boat appeared in the dark mist. A moment later, the light of the torches revealed the monster standing in the center, rowing feverishly with a long paddle.

As with the last time I'd seen Grendel, he wore plated armor as well as an enormous bear's face atop his head with the bear's fur flowing down his back. The bear's mouth was open in a vicious snarl, its eyes as black as the midnight hour. Already tall and bulky, with the added height of the bear head, Grendel was a giant. The torchlight made his shadow even longer and more menacing.

With several last swift strokes, he guided his boat into shallow water, letting the bottom scrape against the rocks lining the shore. When it stuck, he lifted his face skyward and howled like a wounded animal. His face was so overgrown with his matted beard and scraggly hair that his features were indistinguishable. As the guttural cry filled the air, foam dribbled from his open mouth onto his beard.

What had this poor soul been like before he'd turned into a madman? At one time, had he lived a normal life with a wife and perhaps a wee babe? Maybe he'd been a kind and giving neighbor with friends and family. Maybe he'd been a farmer or fisherman or tradesman who earned an honest living. Maybe he'd lived a humble and simple life, never daring to hurt a single soul.

What had happened to turn him into a monster?

With shaking hands, he climbed from his boat and into the lake where he stood ankle deep. He retrieved a double-headed axe from the boat as well as several other frightening weapons I couldn't name. Then he sloshed through the water toward land.

His long shadow fell across the grassy embankment, and he tossed what appeared to be a knife. The blade sliced into the closest sheep, causing it to jump to its feet and squeal in pain. The others around it, sensing the turmoil, rose in confusion and started to run, bleating at one another.

I trembled. When would he notice me? And would he impale me with a weapon like he had the sheep, weakening me before approaching to finish me off?

He stumbled farther up the shore and released another scream with more foaming.

Again, I couldn't keep from thinking about his former life, about the man he'd once been. And my father's words sifted into my conscience: *"Kindness can form the bridge that helps a person cross from pain to peace."*

Had anyone ever shown Grendel kindness? Would such kindness serve as the balm to cover past wounds, or was he too far removed to ever heal and return to a normal life?

From the corner of my vision, I caught a movement along the edge of the arena. The stealthy movement of a man creeping forward, weapons out and poised to kill. The strong, sturdy form and broad shoulders belonged to none other than Vilmar.

My heart stuttered in protest of his being anywhere nearby. Even though I knew I needed his help to kill Grendel, a part of me had hoped the queen would find a way to detain him and keep him from fighting. But I should have known nothing would hold him back. He was a man of honor and valor and determination. Only death itself would stop him.

"No," I whispered, fear for him rushing in to replace all rational thoughts. Now that he was here, I didn't want him to face mortal danger. He was more important than even my own life, and I would gladly suffer and die at the hands of Grendel if I could save Vilmar.

Frantically, I glanced around, searching for a way to keep Grendel from noticing Vilmar.

Grendel rushed with almost superhuman speed into the midst of the sheepfold. With a terrifying roar, he slashed and hacked at the animals, killing them all in mere seconds. From the sacrifices of years past, I knew Grendel's slaughter would soon be over. If there was anything positive about the occasion, it was that the onlookers wouldn't be subjected to the bloodbath for long.

From Vilmar's position, he appeared to be approaching Grendel from behind. Was he hoping to sneak up on him undetected?

It would never work. The grassy area was too wide open without any places for him to hide. If he had any hope of surviving, I would need to draw Grendel's attention.

What could I do to lure him near? Dare I toss my knife and hope to hit him?

As soon as the thought came, I again pictured Grendel as a man like Vilmar, a man with hopes and dreams for a better life, a man with honor and goodness, a man with family who mourned this beast he'd become.

Vilmar crept cautiously away from the stone wall, crouching low but with a nimbleness that spoke of years of training. I had no doubt he was a fierce warrior, a man who could slay countless in battle. But could he really prevail over Grendel as he claimed?

My body tensed as Vilmar came farther into the arena out of the shadows.

Grendel lifted his axe to his mouth and licked the blood now coating it. He sniffed the air before growling and lurching toward the goats. He took one step, then two before he stalled and stiffened, almost as if he sensed Vilmar's presence.

"Leave!" I wanted to shout. "Run away!" But Vilmar would never listen to me, would never leave. I had to distract Grendel and give Vilmar more time.

I opened my mouth to shout at the monster, but another of my father's admonitions wrestled for my attention: "Slay your enemies with the greatest weapon of all: kindness."

Instead of angry words falling from my lips, a familiar psalm came out. It was one I'd sung many times, one that had soothed the thrashing of the fever-ridden or those recovering from an amputation. While I sang it to others, the words and melody oft comforted me.

Now, as the sweet psalm filled the air, I prayed the words would do that again, bring me comfort in my last moments.

At the first notes, Grendel turned his face my direction and sniffed the air once more, this time taking note of my presence in the arena. With the bear head perched above him, I could almost believe the beast was still alive, that its dark eyes were staring straight at me, and that the menacing growl was coming from between the sharp teeth.

His footsteps veered toward me, and fear rose into my throat and threatened to choke off my song. As I forced the melody out, I recalled my father's words again. "Slay your enemy with the greatest weapon of all: kindness."

Vilmar moved more quickly now that I'd distracted Grendel. His features were hard but contained an edge of panic. I sensed he wasn't happy about my drawing Grendel to the table, but I had to fight the only way I truly knew how. Not with a knife, but with a song.

Though my voice wobbled, I sang louder, the words of the ancient verses of praise to God filling the walled pasture.

Vilmar held up his seax, not in a motion of throwing, but what appeared to be a signal. The next instant, another boat floated into the torchlight and rapidly approached the shore. Before the vessel could hit land, a dozen men slipped over the edge and into the water. As the men waded ashore, light glinted off Curly's scraggly red hair.

I noted their familiar faces, all of them from the mine pits, including Vilmar's manservant. Their presence here meant they'd gained their freedom along with Vilmar. How had they all done it?

And now they were in grave danger by coming ashore while Grendel was still raging.

Perhaps if Grendel killed me first, his thirst for blood and death would be sated, and he'd leave the men alone. Despair wrestled deep within. The reality was, even after he slit my throat, he could still turn around and wipe out the men before they had time to raise a weapon in defense.

Coming to the end of the first verse, I hastily continued with the second, praying my voice would drown out the footsteps of the men closing in around Grendel. At the very least, I prayed he would keep his attention upon me. So far, he hadn't veered away. He pushed forward, his feet carrying him until he reached the edge of the stone table.

Then he stopped and peered up at me. And I

shifted my gaze from the bear head to his face, to his eyes. Through dirty strands of hair, dark eyes regarded me. They were wild and bloodshot, full of fury . . . and bewilderment.

Had he not heard singing in so long that he'd forgotten what it was? Or perhaps no one had offered him kindness, so he didn't recognize it. Was it possible he'd been treated as beast for all these years and had lost hope of ever being anything else?

I continued to sing, coming to the end of the second stanza and moving into the third. As I did, I kept hold of his gaze and lifted the song higher. He watched my face intently, his breathing ragged, foam still gathering at his lips.

Slowly I lowered myself until I was kneeling, my face level with his.

He grunted but didn't move. Instead, some of the fury in his eyes seemed to fade.

Taking courage from the fact that he hadn't yet sliced me open, I cautiously extended my hand.

Vilmar and the others were only two dozen paces away. They fanned out in a circle, clearly intending to trap Grendel. Several of them carried between them a net made of chain mail, while the others held at the ready an assortment of weapons.

Your knife, Vilmar mouthed while making a slicing motion at his neck.

I knew very well what Vilmar was instructing me to do. He wanted me to use Grendel's moment of weakness to my advantage, to plunge my knife into the artery exactly the way he'd shown me dozens of times during my training.

But my knife was still sheathed beneath my gown,

and right now I'd extended to Grendel kindness, perhaps in a way no one ever had. He glanced down at my hand, then up at my eyes. His confusion was heartbreaking.

I reached out my hand farther, and he grunted an almost worried sound. I tried to offer him a smile of assurance and friendship. Then as his gaze returned to my face, I did the unthinkable. I cupped his cheek.

He stiffened and trembled. For a second I worried I'd gone too far. But as I battled a moment of fear, I forced myself to remain in place. I would rather die wielding kindness than my knife.

Vilmar and the men closed in, which meant I had little time left. I pressed Grendel's dirty, grizzled cheek and hoped I'd conveyed to him that I saw past the monster to the man he could yet become.

At a soft clinking of the net, Grendel spun away from me. In that instant, Vilmar and the other men sprang upon him, tossing the chain-mail net over him and wrestling him to the ground. He roared with new fury and fought back with the force of a dozen bears.

"Don't kill him!" I shouted, trying to make myself heard over the yelling and Grendel's commotion.

No one paid me heed. They were too intent upon subduing Grendel and keeping him from fighting his way free of the net.

I stood, closed my eyes, and once again sang, this time the lullaby Vilmar had shared while we worked to save ourselves when we were trapped in the mine. I didn't recall all the words, but the tune was one that was familiar in any language, one I hoped Grendel would know.

As my melody rose in volume, Grendel ceased his

flailing, letting himself fall to his knees on the ground, the bear head knocked off his head. He craned to see me, and this time, through the chain-mail net, I glimpsed his eyes. Though still bloodshot and wild, the confusion was gone and in its place was sadness. I didn't have time to read the sadness and discover what it meant. For in the next instant, one of the men brought a bludgeon down upon Grendel's head, causing him to slump to the ground unconscious.

Vilmar issued sharp instructions, and the men hurriedly worked to bind Grendel's feet and hands with chains before they wrapped him once more in the chain-mail net. Vilmar shouted further commands to the closest of the queen's guards—something about securing a cage.

Only then, did I become aware of the cheering from the audience above. I glanced up, and many were hugging and openly weeping, so great was their relief.

One stood apart from the others. Having risen from her throne, Queen Margery held herself rigidly, her fingers gripping her goblet so tightly that it shook. Though the darkness of the midnight hour provided some cover, the cold anger in her expression was clear enough. We'd put an end to her cruel custom, and now, without the fairest maiden's heart, she would have no way to continue her alchemy.

As her attention shifted from the placid Grendel to the princely Vilmar and then to me, our gazes connected.

I rose, straightened my shoulders, and lifted my chin, unwilling to cower before her any longer. I'd accomplished what I set out to do, but in a way I never anticipated. Wasn't that the way of kindness? That it brought results in the manner least expected? I could only pray that, in heaven above, my father was looking down upon me proudly.

The queen stared fiercely even as she called out to one of the knights standing guard near her throne. He stepped forward, bowed, and leaned in for her instructions. As he straightened, he followed her gaze to me and then to Vilmar. He hesitated only a moment before he nodded and strode away.

She wouldn't dare arrest us tonight, would she? Not with all these people looking on and lauding us for capturing Grendel? What explanation could she possibly give everyone for taking us captive?

I wanted to toss aside my fears, but I already knew what the queen was capable of doing when threatened. And I suspected we wouldn't be safe until we were far away from her clutches.

Chapter
19

VILMAR

MY INSIDES QUAVERED UNCONTROLLABLY, THOUGH I ATTEMPTED to remain outwardly composed. As several guards brought ashore the iron cage I'd asked to have on hand, I kept one eye on Gabriella, now freed from her chains and standing beside Curly. Her interaction with the berserker had been too risky. And I hadn't yet recovered from helplessly watching her kneel before the madman.

Of course, I couldn't deny her plan to calm the berserker had worked better than anything I'd construed. In fact, she was brilliant to sing and lull him into a state of trust. What I didn't understand was why she hadn't slit his throat the way I'd taught her. Instead, she'd reached out and touched the madman, almost as if she felt compassion instead of fear.

She was fortunate Grendel hadn't reached out in return and sliced her open. I had expected it at any moment, was ready to throw my seax at the first sight of his. I held back only because I knew the best way to defeat him was to capture him beneath the net of chain mail and hinder his movements. Even then, our fight would have been brutal and deadly, if not for Gabriella's beautiful voice soothing him again.

An ache pulsed through my chest at how close I'd come to losing her. I wanted to race over, scold her for taking such a risk, then crush her in an embrace and never let her go. But I held myself back. For now, I had to make sure Grendel was secured, caged, and on his way back to Scania.

I'd previously sent word to Lord Kennard to secure means of transportation. I didn't want to leave any details to the queen for fear she'd purposefully set the berserker free to serve her own purposes again. In fact, I planned to accompany the berserker back to Scania, and I wouldn't rest until Grendel was locked away in the dungeons.

"Use the extra chains to bind him to the cage," I called to the soldiers now hefting him behind the metal bars. Faces pale with fear, they worked quickly, rushing to finish their contact with the berserker before he roused and roared out again, more furious than before.

Though my father's capture of the other berserkers had been long ago, I still recalled how one had torn himself free from a rope of hemp and a cage of wood. Iron was the only material strong enough to contain berserkers when they were raging.

The soldiers closed the cage and secured it with several more chains. With the madman finally locked away, the thick iron gate at the side of the arena began to clank as it rose. It protected a stone stairway that led to the cliffs above, the only way in and out of the arena except for the lake.

I attempted to breathe out the tension still holding me in its vise. We were safe. Neither Gabriella nor any other maiden need fear the yearly sacrifice ever again.

"Congratulations, Your Highness." Lord Kennard ducked under the still-rising gate and onto the grassy field. He and another nobleman skirted the dead sheep and veered toward me. "The people above are awaiting a word from you."

The cheering, whistling, and clapping had subsided. But from what I could see, the crowds on the cliffs had grown in size, not diminished.

"News of Grendel's demise is being shouted from the rooftops," Lord Kennard said, as though reading my question. "And the townspeople have come out of hiding to witness the glorious occasion. Hundreds are gathering above to see their heroes."

Upon reaching me, he knelt, as did his companion. I dipped my head in acknowledgment of their respect. I could no longer conceal my identity as a Prince of Scania. From the moment I'd revealed myself at the ball, apparently the word had spread even to Curly and the other men from the mine, who'd bowed before me when I'd met with them to make our plans.

Of the men, only Curly had spoken to me in the same manner he always had, as if my royalty was of no consequence. I realized then that I would not miss the kingship, that I could grow accustomed to remaining a simple prince. Mikkel would make a worthy king in my stead. I need not worry about the country's welfare under his rule.

My experience in the mines had stripped away everything and shown me just how conceited I truly was. My whole life, I'd placed too much pride in myself and my connections with important nobility and the Lagting. I'd striven to please people and gain their acceptance for my own betterment rather than for what I could do for them.

And now, I knew that even if being the slave of all was difficult, serving others brought more contentment than being served. Was it possible that in sacrificing, one gained more than one gave? That only in laying down one's life could one truly learn to live?

My attention strayed to Gabriella, still at Curly's side. Her life was proof of that. She gave of herself day after day in countless ways to others, and she never ran out of herself. In fact, she seemed to have a boundless supply of kindness that had somehow spilled over to Grendel.

Lord Kennard rose, and though a smile graced his face, his eyes were much too solemn. "I suggest that you address the people, Your Highness. If the queen hears their praise, she may delay your arrest."

"Arrest?" My gaze darted to the throne, but the queen was no longer in her spot. "On what charges?"

Even as the question left my lips, I knew the answer. Word of the slave revolt had reached her. Maybe she'd even known of it before I made my way into the pit to fight Grendel but hadn't expected me to live. Now that I had, she planned to use the revolt against me.

"She is telling her loyal guards you must be arrested because you set the worst criminals in the kingdom free from slavery." Lord Kennard lowered his voice to a whisper. "Her guards are even now waiting in the stairwell for you to pass through so they might secretly take you away."

I glanced through the open gate. A torch in the wall glowed brightly, revealing the tunnel that led to the stairwell. "If I rally the people to my side, then you think she will have no choice but to let me leave this place as a free man?"

"We can only pray so. At least for the time being, until she has time to sway their opinion against you." He lowered his voice. "If she lays hold of you, Your Highness, I fear you will never leave Warwick alive."

I feared the same. Not only for myself but also for Gabriella. The queen would find a way to silence us both.

"After you speak to the people and while everyone is celebrating, you must sneak away across the lake and find your way out of Warwick secretly."

I nodded my assent. Perhaps I would suggest feasting and celebrating all night long right here in the field. And when the rejoicing was at its height, I could slip away unnoticed with Gabriella.

But with so dangerous a madman still alive, how could I run away? "I must ensure Grendel's safe removal from this country. I cannot rest until I know he's returned to my homeland."

"As you requested, the arrangements for his transport are well under way, Your Highness. And I shall accompany the beast in your stead." The seriousness of Lord Kennard's expression told me he would indeed guard the berserker well and do everything within his power to rid Warwick of the menace. "I shall immediately direct a missive to King Christian and call upon him for assistance. He will surely send his strongest warriors to aid in the conveyance of the monster."

Yes, my father would help. But would his men be able to arrive before the queen could interfere? "You will need to be well armed."

Lord Kennard nodded to his companion, who stood a respectful distance away. "I have even now enlisted the aid of several noblemen and their knights."

Despite his assurances, I hesitated. Something inside

me protested running and hiding from the queen.

"Please, Your Highness. You have made a mortal enemy of the queen, and she will seek retribution for your interference here in Warwick."

She'd likely hunt down all the men who'd fought with me tonight. What would become of them if I left them behind and ran away to Scania? And was it even possible for me to escape to my homeland? The queen would most likely catch me before I had the chance to secure passage off the Great Isle.

At the chanting of her name, Gabriella waved up at the people, earning more cheering and applause. Attired in her elegant emerald gown, one worthy of a princess, she was most certainly the fairest maiden, especially now, after facing the madman.

And she was still my betrothed.

Though the betrothal ceremony had been a last and desperate effort to protect her, I didn't take my vows lightly. I'd given my word to marry her, and I would—no matter the long-term consequences and estrangement I brought upon myself from my father and the Lagting.

The truth was, I didn't just have myself to think about in the coming dangerous days. I had her now too. I had to do whatever would keep her the safest, and the best option at this point was to find a place where we could hide. Perhaps we could escape to Mercia with the other slaves.

"Thank you for the warning regarding the queen's motives, Lord Kennard. You took a great risk in delivering the news to me. If you should ever find yourself in trouble, you will always be welcome in Scania."

He bowed his head. "Thank you, Your Highness. Warwick is my home, and even when the country is at its worst, I trust that the Sovereign Lord has put me here to carry out his work, whatever that might be."

I nodded. Then before the queen grew impatient and decided to send her soldiers out of the stairwell after me, I strode forward toward Gabriella. As I took my place next to her, I reached for her hand.

She glanced at me in surprise.

"The queen's knights are waiting in the stairwell to capture us," I said, as I smiled up at the cliffs and raised my arm with Gabriella's in a sign of solidarity and victory. "We must delay her efforts by garnering the support of the people."

The crowd cheered louder.

As Gabriella's lips rose, her smile didn't reach her eyes. Her fingers clasped mine, and I could feel her tremble. I prayed that this time, I could find a way to free her from the queen's grasp once and for all.

Several enormous bonfires lit the grassy area now filled with hundreds of people who were feasting, dancing, and celebrating Grendel's capture. After speaking again to Lord Kennard and finalizing more plans, the nobleman had taken Grendel in his cage away by boat. I'd reluctantly watched them disappear into the night.

For now, my new mission was to escape with Gabriella. During the past hour of revelry, I'd made my intentions known to Ty and Curly along with my instructions. They'd dispersed into the crowds, the same way I hoped to do.

Though I stayed close to Gabriella and kept her in my

line of vision as we mingled, I tried to remain calm in case the queen or her spies were watching. I didn't want them discovering how nervous I was and suspect I was plotting a getaway.

As the hour crept closer to dawn, we had to make our move. I caught Gabriella's gaze and nodded. When the fiddles struck up the melody of the next dance, she approached one of the slaves from the mine. They began to twirl in the steps of a folk dance, and she allowed the momentum to take her near the shore where Ty and Curly were already waiting.

As the couple stepped into the shadows, the slave rotated farther into the darkness with Gabriella, and a moment later reappeared with a peasant woman. Though the new woman in her peasant garments didn't look anything like Gabriella, hopefully no one would notice right away.

I waited several moments before I casually edged toward the opposite side, since it was too risky for me to depart in the same vicinity as Gabriella. I slipped into the dark shadows near the wall. After glancing over my shoulder to see if anyone had noticed my exit, I waded into the water. Already having taken off the queen's armor, I moved swiftly, with naught but my weapons to weigh me down.

Though I'd known the lake was fed by mountain streams, the water was colder than I'd expected. Nevertheless, I was accustomed to the frigid temperature of the fjords in Scania and had learned to swim in them from the time I could walk. Thus, I plunged deeper and dove below the surface.

When I emerged, I was far enough from the shore that no one would be able to spot me. Using the bonfires as my guide, I swam hard, not knowing how much time we had before the queen's men noticed we were gone and came looking for us.

"There," came Curly's loud whisper. "He's there."

I propelled myself toward the faint outline of the bobbing boat. Within minutes, Curly and Ty pulled me over the side. Before I had the chance to shake the water from my body, they were already rowing swiftly into deeper water.

In the darkness, I groped against the hull to find another set of oars and bumped into Gabriella instead.

"Here," she whispered, wrapping something over my shoulders and around my torso. "It's not nearly large enough for you, but it'll do for now."

"Thank you," I said, my teeth chattering and my body numb from cold.

I dragged the cloak about me, not sure whose it was or where it had come from but grateful nonetheless for Gabriella's thoughtfulness. I sensed her nearby and wanted to grab her into an embrace and reassure myself that she was now safe.

But to do so would be premature. We had a difficult journey ahead, especially once the queen sent out her best knights to track us.

I found another set of oars and dipped them in, adding my strength and speed to Curly's and Ty's. Within minutes, the laughter and singing and music faded until the only sound was the rhythmic slap of our rowing.

Chapter
20

Gabriella

Weariness had become my constant companion. I simply clung to the pommel and prayed I wouldn't fall off my mount.

Curly led the way, urging us onward, ever higher and faster. From the tense glances he tossed over his shoulder to the darkening forest behind us, I suspected the queen's men were getting closer as the evening gave way to dusk. They'd been gaining ground all day, although I didn't know how Curly could tell.

Our trip by boat across Wraith Lake had been short. When we reached the shore, the men chopped up the boat and pushed it out into the water where it sank, destroying evidence we'd been there. Then we hiked for several leagues before we came upon the horses laden with supplies and food Lord Kennard had arranged for us. The walking had wasted precious time according to Curly. And ever since then, we'd been attempting to outdistance our pursuers.

If only the guards hadn't noticed our disappearance

from the festivities until morning... As it was, apparently someone had discovered our absence sooner rather than later, and the chase began.

Now Curly guided us deep into the foothills on trails only visible to his trained eye and into places I'd never known existed in Warwick—wild land with majestic waterfalls and rushing rivers, along with smaller cascading waterfalls and tributaries. If I hadn't been so tired, I might have appreciated the grandeur more thoroughly, but I could only think of staying awake and in my saddle.

I'd overheard the men saying that we would stick to the desolate trails as we worked our way north into Inglewood Forest with the hope of eventually meeting up with the other runaway slaves Molly was leading into hiding. The trip would take several more days of hard riding and would tax our mounts to the limit, especially with having to traverse up and down the hills.

What the men left unsaid was that we wouldn't make half that distance if we didn't somehow shake Queen Margery's knights from our trail. I managed a look behind me at Vilmar. His body was rigid with determination, and his face tense with frustration that we weren't making more progress.

Though he didn't say so, he was exhausted. His features contained a haggardness that hadn't been there previously. How long had it been since he'd slept? Since before leading the slave revolt?

The men had shared with me more details regarding their getaway from the Gemstone Mountains—how they'd outwitted the guards, freed all the slaves, and fled with their lives intact. I'd been awed by their bravery. Curly gave Vilmar and Ty all the credit, indicating that if not for their swift ability to silence the tower guards, the escape would have been more dangerous. Certainly many would have died.

Although Vilmar had answered my questions about his Testing and his country's custom in choosing their next king, he'd been strangely quiet all day. I suspected he was preoccupied with worry over the transfer of Grendel back to Scania. He'd spoken tersely with Ty about it on several occasions. Had he given up his plans to escort Grendel, so he'd be free to act as my bodyguard?

The farther we rode, the guiltier I felt for dragging Vilmar so deeply into Warwick's problems. They weren't his to worry about, and yet here he was accompanying me and making sure I was safe. I also blamed myself for his failure to finish his Testing, even though he insisted he willingly chose to end his part of the competition to become king.

Did he feel bound to me because of our betrothal?

His words from last night during the dance came back to me: *"I want no one else but you."* He'd spoken them with such sincerity, and yet I couldn't allow myself to dwell on the affection. We'd been on the precipice of death. And we'd spoken and acted as if we had no tomorrow.

Because Vilmar was a man of honor, he would never go against his word or promise. Nonetheless, I didn't want him staying with me out of obligation to a vow he made because he hoped to save me. Instead, I wanted to give him back his freedom so he could restore himself into the good graces of his people and yet have a chance at being king. Once they heard of his daring deeds, they'd surely approve.

I'd grown more convinced with each passing hour that I must cut him free as soon as I had the chance to speak privately with him. I would reassure him that Curly could lead me to Inglewood Forest. And there I would establish a new life with the friends I'd made in the mines.

The truth was, I'd never be able to return to my home in Rockland. I would never be secure as long as the queen lived. And I couldn't ask Vilmar to join me in that kind of existence, no matter how much I'd grown to care about him.

Curly led us down a mossy bank toward another river, the beautiful waterfall cascading from the rocky ledge upriver. When he reached the middle of the river, he reined in his horse and pointed toward the waterfall. "It's time to be hiding. We'll take cover there until the queen's men give up the search."

"Where?" I saw nothing but the waterfall and the wet granite it flowed over.

"Do ye trust me?" He offered me the first smile all day.

"Of course I do."

The river was fast moving and frigid. As I guided my horse upriver, the water surged against us, soaking into my fragile slippers as well as into the hem of my gown. The closer we drew, the stronger the current, until I feared it might take us back down to where we'd begun.

Curly halted a few feet from the spray. It rained against us, and if I'd had any hope of staying dry, I lost it.

"We need to go through," he called to us above the

roar of the water. He nudged his horse directly into the pouring stream. He ducked his head and hunched his back, letting the water pound against him. A moment later he was gone. Ty did the same, disappearing into the mist.

Swallowing my trepidation, I urged my steed forward. The creature balked, tossing his head and snorting his fear. But at the slap of Vilmar's riding whip to his haunches, he lurched into the water flow. For several seconds the water drenched me, and I felt as though I were drowning under a pummeling of ice.

But as I passed through to the other side, I blinked the water out of my eyes and found that my horse was standing in a calm, shallow pool. Straight ahead, Curly and Ty had led their mounts out of the water into a dark cavern. They'd dismounted and Curly was already in the process of guiding his horse farther away from the waterfall. Next to me, Vilmar spluttered, wiping his eyes and combing wet strands of hair off his face.

"We can tie up the horses here," Curly said. "And then we'll hike back in where we can start a fire and dry out."

"Won't the queen's guards see the light from our fire?" Vilmar scanned our surroundings with his keen gaze, likely not missing a single detail.

"We have a short while before darkness. After that, aye, we'll need to be extinguishing the flames for the night."

While Ty and Vilmar tended our horses and speared for fish in the pool, Curly disappeared through the waterfall to gather wood, staying in the water along the banks so the hunting dogs wouldn't be able to track our scent. A short while later, he plunged back through the waterfall, keeping the majority of wood dry by shielding it with an oiled blanket from amongst our supplies.

He made quick work of starting a small fire, but even when the heat began to fill the cavern, I couldn't stop shaking. As Vilmar approached with several fish on the tip of his sword, his brows furrowed as he took me in. "You're freezing."

"I shall warm soon enough." I tried to keep my voice cheerful, but the cold made it wobbly.

Vilmar handed his sword to Ty who followed behind him, his spear stacked with fish too. "If you strip to your chemise," Vilmar lifted his chain mail over his head, "your garments will dry quicker."

Mortified at his suggestion, I retreated a step. "I cannot—"

"We shall turn our backs and give you privacy." He continued to shed his own garments, dropping his weapons belt and then raising his tunic.

At the sight of his bare chest, I was the one to spin and face the darkness of the cavern. My face was suddenly hot, though I knew not why. I'd witnessed various states of undress during my months at the mine. Our close living quarters had made modesty difficult.

At the crunch of steps directly behind me, I stiffened.

"Gabriella," he said softly, "you won't make it through the night in your wet garments. You must at least take off the outer layers and allow them to dry."

He was right. And truthfully, my chemise underneath was modest and of good, sturdy material. I wasn't sure why I was hesitating. "Very well," I said just as softly in return. "I shall go farther into the darkness and undress."

I didn't wait for his response and instead walked several paces until I was hidden in the shadows. I made quick work of shedding the emerald gown the duchess had arranged for me to wear to the Choosing Ball. Though it was undeniably beautiful, as the heavy, wet weight fell from my shoulders, I felt as though I'd been set free. I stepped out and kicked it across the cave floor. For the first time in months I was truly free from the burdens I'd been carrying. Grendel was captured. The sacrifices to him were over. And the fairest maidens in the land could now rejoice.

I'd accomplished the impossible, and now I could rejoice too.

I tried to smile. Instead, I shuddered, but this time not from the cold. This time the shudder came from a place deep inside, a place that had somehow filled with love for Vilmar though I'd tried not to let it.

I loved him. The realization rose swiftly and painfully, and I would have cried out except that I cupped my hand over my mouth to catch it.

"Come back to the warmth of the fire, Gabriella," he beckoned. "We have no time to waste in our efforts to dry out."

I wanted to tell him I couldn't come back, that we had to part ways. This was the moment to do so. I needed to free him. To cling to him would be entirely selfish of me.

I glanced to where Ty was roasting the fish above the crackling flames. "Your Highness, we need to speak." But even as I tried to force the words out, I couldn't contain my shivering.

He stalked over to me, and before I could protest, he scooped me up and carried me to the fire. Though I was mortified to be cocooned against his bare chest, the warmth of his flesh seeped into me. Upon reaching the flames, instead of releasing me, he lowered himself to the ground until I was sitting on his lap. The heat from the flames toasted me from the front, and his body provided warmth from behind.

Still embarrassed by the intimate position as well as his bare chest, I conceded that his efforts were noble and naught more. Without his warmth, I would have frozen, and he knew it. Nevertheless, I didn't allow myself to relax against him and instead held myself rigidly. Moments later, when Ty offered us cooked fish, I made a move to leave the comfort and warmth of Vilmar's hold, but he curled his arm around my waist. "Stay," he whispered.

At the plea in his voice, I made no further effort to distance myself. Instead, I gratefully relished each bite of fish. As the warmth of the meal settled inside, I closed my eyes, too tired to keep them open. Within seconds, I fell asleep.

Something jolted me awake. I was surprised at the warmth surrounding me. In fact, I was warmer than I'd been in a very long time. I started to stretch but then startled at the tightening of thick arms around me.

My eyes flew open to utter darkness, and memories of the previous day rushed into my consciousness— fleeing from the queen's guards, the long day of traveling, and then hiding behind the waterfall. The steady cascade of the water told me we were still in the secret cave. But our fire was doused and everyone was silent.

I attempted to move again, but lips pressed against my cheek, halting me. I was suddenly aware of my position—Vilmar was leaning against the cave wall, I was reclining against his chest, his legs outstretched on either side of mine, and his arms wrapped around me, covering me like a cloak. Thankfully, he was no longer shirtless. Nevertheless, our predicament was less than proper.

Although my chemise was still damp, I'd dried out enough I could sit by myself. To linger longer with Vilmar would certainly be indecent.

I tried to sit up, but he bent in, his lips brushing my cheek once more before finding my ear. "Don't move. Soldiers are searching nearby."

Immediately, I stilled. In the distance beyond the sheet of running water, I caught the faint glimmer of light. Torches? My pulse sped with fear. "Do you think they will discover our hiding place?"

"Curly insists that only he and his fellow hunters know about this cave," Vilmar whispered.

"But the torches are so near. What if they have learned about it?"

"If they come inside, we shall fight them. Curly and Ty are standing guard on either side of the fall."

"No. I shall not allow you to fight for me again."

The soft exhalations of his breathing ceased.

"You have already done too much," I rushed to explain. "You have put your life in jeopardy for me too many times, and I cannot allow you to do so any more."

"The queen seeks my life as much as she does yours."

"Because of me." My whisper grew more adamant. "I have brought danger upon you."

"I have made my own choices—"

"If not for me, you would never have left the mine pits."

"If not for you, I wouldn't have learned how to be a better man."

How was he a better man because of me? He'd already been noble and gallant. I shook my head. "I have led to your demise. You ended your Testing because of me."

"Maybe at first I wanted to abandon my Testing so I could save you. But in the end, I did it to free everyone from slavery. I realize now that was my destiny, to lay down my life as a ransom for many, and I would have done it with or without you."

My racing thoughts paused. I, too, sensed he would have freed the slaves. That's the kind of man he was. My leaving the mine had merely spurred him to do it sooner. "Nevertheless, I release you from the betrothal and any obligation to me."

"You don't have the power to do so." His whisper turned hard. "The vows we took are binding."

"They were spoken under duress; therefore, you are not beholden to me."

He shifted, his body tensing against mine. "No one can force me, even under the greatest duress, to make promises I don't intend to keep."

"But, Your Highness—"

He pressed a kiss against my ear, cutting off my words and thoughts. I reveled in his nearness and the

227

echo of his breath in the hollow of my ear. After a moment, he lifted away. "Do not call me that ever again." His request was harsh.

"Call you what?"

"By my title."

"But that is my whole point." I twisted around, wishing I could see his face. But the darkness was too thick. "You are a prince. You deserve a woman of your equal, not a poor woman, a nobody—"

His mouth descended upon mine, powerfully and fully, giving me no chance to protest any further and sweeping me away in a current of desire. I raised my hand to his cheek and kissed him back, no longer able to contain my love.

An admonition tolled like a bell somewhere at the back of my mind. I was being selfish and needed to let him go. But as he slid a hand to my cheek, then neck, my love for him swelled and drowned out the clanging.

A moment later he broke away, leaving me gasping for breath. "I shall have you as my wife and no other for as long as I live." His whisper rang with both passion and determination.

I closed my eyes and basked in the kiss still lingering upon my lips. But even as I considered giving myself over to him, I forced myself to try one more time to sever the bond between us. "I have made a mortal enemy of the queen. She will never stop seeking to silence me. If you align yourself with me, then she will consider you her enemy too."

"She already sees me as an enemy for capturing Grendel."

"That is the crux of the problem." My voice rose, only to receive a shushing warning from Ty and Curly.

I swallowed my desperation and lowered my tone. "If I stay with you, she will have more reason to hate Scania and perhaps even seek retaliation. But if you leave me and return to your homeland, Scania may eventually be able to restore peace with Warwick. Surely, your father and all his advisors would want you to seek Scania's good over your own?"

Before he could respond, a shout came from the river beyond the waterfall and torchlight flickered nearer. Vilmar released me and was on his feet in an instant with his weapons drawn.

Chapter 21

VILMAR

GABRIELLA'S QUESTION ECHOED IN MY MIND AS I BRACED MYSELF for another battle, this time against the queen's men. *"Surely, your father and all his advisors would want you to seek Scania's good over your own?"*

For as long as I could remember, I'd lived to impress my father and the Lagting. Over time I'd earned their favor as well as that of the general populace. But all along, had I sought my own glory? Was that what my Testing needed to reveal?

Beside me, I could hear Gabriella rising. I shifted my sword to my opposite hand and then reached out for her, guiding her behind me where I could guard her against any soldier who might attempt to capture her.

Yes, she was right that our union would be a blemish upon Scania and ruin any possibility of maintaining peace with Warwick. After I'd led the slave revolt and captured Grendel, there was little peace left anyway.

The person I used to be would have taken any amount of peace at any cost in order to please others and make myself more appealing. But I didn't want the easy path to self-glory any longer. I wouldn't abandon Gabriella, and neither would I bring more conflict to Scania. If I must live the rest of my earthly days in hiding and obscurity and never resume my life of privilege, then so be it.

The torchlight came from along both sides of the riverbank and flamed brighter. I tensed and prayed the soldiers wouldn't be able to see behind the waterfall to our hiding place.

Gabriella inched closer, as though seeking my refuge. And once again, as when I'd kissed her, an overwhelming surge of emotions threatened to undo me. This time I had no doubt what the emotion was. Love. I loved her. Loved her deeply and desperately.

Garbled voices from the other side of the waterfall filtered inside, much too close. I held myself motionless, as did Ty and Curly. Thankfully, our horses were resting where we'd tied them earlier, too exhausted to sound any alarm.

While I didn't want to fight anyone tonight, I was prepared to battle the queen for the rest of my life if I had to. I would do it for Gabriella and anyone else Margery tried to wrongly harm. Perhaps that was my life mission— to live humbly and be slave to all who needed assistance.

The lights flamed against the cascading water. Gabriella leaned into my back. I could feel her heartbeat pulsing against my flesh. I reached for her again until I found her hand. I intertwined my fingers with hers and hoped she could understand my message. Henceforth, we would face whatever came our way. Together.

Her fingers tightened within mine. Was she agreeing to the same? She laid her head against my back, her cheek resting there securely. The touch, as when I'd held her earlier, set my skin ablaze. I'd needed no fire for warming then, nor did I now.

Shouts from farther down the hill seemed to draw the attention of the soldiers at the waterfall. I held my breath as they shifted. When the torchlight began to bob away, the air spilled from my lungs, and the tension eased from my shoulders.

Apparently sensing the change in my stance, Gabriella started to back away. I spun before she could move too far. I dropped my weapons, wrapped my arms around her, and drew her near again. I wished for light so I could see her face, but I said the words regardless. "I have but one desire left in my life. And that is to love you all my days."

At the mention of the word *love*, she sucked in a rapid breath.

"I love you, Gabriella." I wished I could find a way to express just how much I loved her, but I guessed that was what marriage was all about—taking a lifetime to show love in small and great ways every day.

"No, you cannot," she protested, although weakly.

"There's nothing you can do to change my love. Not now. Nor ever." I bent down and kissed the top of her head, the silky strands of her hair reminding me what a beautiful woman she was both inside and out. "No matter where we live or what life may bring, I would be the most fortunate man in all the world to earn your affection in return. Will you let me try?"

She shook her head. "You have no need to try."

"Please, my lady. I beg you—"

Her fingertips against my mouth halted my plea. An instant later, her lips replaced her fingers in a tentative but earnest kiss, one that left me as powerless and weak as all the others she'd given me.

When she broke away, she brushed my cheek tenderly. "You have no need to try to earn my affection, because you already have it. You have all my love and will have it forever and beyond."

I reached for her hand and moved it to my lips, kissing her palm, which only made me want to kiss her longer. I resisted and lowered her hand. "Then no more talk of parting ways?"

"'Tis selfish of me when I know I ought to set you free—"

"I am free." For the first time in my life, I truly felt it. The pressure of pleasing and performing and keeping peace was gone. "Together we'll be free to serve the people around us and heap upon them as much kindness as we can give."

"I like that plan." Her tone hinted at a smile.

"Then we shall be married the first chance we have with the first priest we meet." The light of the queen's men had disappeared, leaving the blackness and silence of night in its stead. We would likely need to stay hidden away in our cave for several more days before the knights gave up searching the area and returned to the queen. I didn't want to wait that long to marry Gabriella, but I wouldn't put us at risk for my own impatience.

"I'm a priest." Ty moved away from the entrance and skirted toward us. As always, he'd listened to everything I'd spoken. And this was one time I was glad he'd done so. "I guess that means you must be married now."

"Now?" I couldn't contain a shiver of pleasure. "Perhaps Gabriella would like to wait until we reach a chapel?"

"Now is fine." Her voice was low but with a note of eagerness that made me smile.

"Good," Ty said. "Then as your chaperone, I'll no longer need to worry about how to tactfully implore His Highness to refrain from any further kissing of the lady."

I grinned. "Yes, of course we want to make your duty easier if we possibly can."

"I think Your Highness is putting me out of a job altogether." From the kindness in Ty's tone, I suspected he understood how the challenges of the past months had brought about my inner transformation. And he was pleased with it.

"It's mighty clear God brought ye to each other." Curly now joined us in the cavern. "Never met two kinder souls, and if any deserve happiness, it be ye two."

"You shall have your chance at happiness, Curly," Gabriella said. "We shall reach the others. And then Ty can marry you and Molly straight away."

"I be praying so," he whispered thickly. "That I do."

Curly had been willing to sacrifice much on behalf of Gabriella and me. In fact, he'd left before he had the opportunity to marry Molly, knowing he might never see her again. I, too, could only pray someday erelong he'd have the chance at happiness.

Today, now, was my chance. I drew Gabriella into the crook of my arm eagerly, and Ty took his place in front of us. As we spoke our vows to each other, ones nearly identical to our betrothal vows, my heart swelled with both peace and joy. This was where I wanted to be, by this woman's side and nowhere else.

"The Lord mercifully, with his favor, look upon you," Ty concluded, "and so fill you with all spiritual benediction and grace, that you may so live together in this life, that in the world to come you may have life everlasting. Amen."

"Amen," I whispered with the others.

"Now you may kiss your bride, Your Highness," Ty said, "anytime and anyplace you wish."

"And as long as I wish?" I drew Gabriella into my arms.

"Now that is something only your bride can determine."

I framed my bride's face, feeling her lips curve into a smile. "How long may I kiss you, my beloved bride?"

Her smile widened. "Most fervently now and forever."

Chapter 22

Queen Margery

"They vanished." I repeated the words of the commander, tapping my fingers against the armrest of my throne, the jewels from the rings glittering brilliantly.

"Yes, Your Majesty." His voice wavered, laden with fear, and rightfully so. At the foot of my dais, he was close enough I could see the stark despair in his eyes. "They vanished without a trace."

"Without a trace." I kept my voice as calm as I could. It was a technique I'd learned instilled more fear than when I erupted into one of my rages. "How is such a thing even possible?"

"My scouts, along with my best tracking dogs, have searched for over a week. But they have left us no trail." He glanced behind him to the dozen or more of his best knights who'd been tasked with bringing me Prince Vilmar and Lady Gabriella. Defeat lay upon every shoulder and creased every face.

The commander had likely pushed the knights

hard, giving them little opportunity to eat or sleep. I had no doubt he'd swiftly punished any who slackened their duties. Nevertheless, he and the men had failed me.

I thrummed my fingers again, my long nails clicking and filling the silence that had settled over the great hall.

"My speculation," the commander continued tentatively, "is that they made their way by river to the coast and have by now left the country altogether."

"Commander, you know I do not like speculating." In fact, over the years of practicing alchemy, I'd grown to despise all the speculating involved in the process.

"I beg your forgiveness, Your Majesty." He knelt and bowed his head. "My knights and I do not deserve your mercy for our failure, but I beg you to give us another chance to search for the prince and his lady."

I straightened my already rigid spine and head, enjoying the swish of the diamonds studded throughout my hair. Soon I would have jewels of gold. Very soon.

"Please, Your Majesty. We shall turn our searches to the coast and commandeer every vessel—"

"No." I twisted one of my pearl rings, admiring the iridescent white. I waited several long moments, allowing the soldiers as well as the other nobility present in my great hall to squirm. They needed to fear what I would do. Such fear was healthy for the people and kept them subservient.

"As you have failed in capturing the leaders of the slave revolt," I finally said, "I should have each of you hanged, drawn, and quartered."

Beads of sweat broke out on the commander's

forehead beneath his hood of chain mail. Since Midsummer's Eve, the people had hailed Prince Vilmar and Lady Gabriella as heroes for subduing Grendel.

However, I'd steadily undermined the two, spreading word about how they'd led a slave revolt and freed dozens of dangerous criminals who were now roaming throughout Warwick causing terror. In order to perpetuate the tale, I'd released the vilest and most violent criminals from my dungeons and given them leave to strike fear in the hearts of the people at will.

Day by day, as more violence and crime spread throughout the land, the tide of opinion had begun to shift so people no longer praised Prince Vilmar and Lady Gabriella quite so loudly. I'd instructed my most trusted servants to plant seeds of discord, and now the people were complaining they'd been rescued from one terror only to be besieged by another.

"I shall show you mercy this day. Instead of rightly punishing you for failing me, I shall instead give you another task by which you can atone for your mistakes."

"Thank you, Your Majesty." The commander bowed his head again, but not before I caught sight of his relief. "We are most grateful. Your word shall be our command."

I rose from my throne, and my gown trimmed in rubies clinked against the marble floor. Anger rushed through me as it had since Grendel's capture and the realization that I would no longer be able to continue making jewels. After all, I couldn't simply rush out and kill beautiful maidens, not without a valid excuse. Doing so would incite the people to revolt, especially when the rumblings of rebellion were already spreading.

Henceforth, the time had come for me to change my tactics and accomplish the one thing no one else had ever been able to do—make gold. I'd been the one to labor tirelessly with my alchemists for years to decipher the ultimate ingredient. Now history would forever remember me for my discovery. And for my power and wealth. Once I made the gold and others learned of my capability, I'd be able to command the allegiance of kings and kingdoms far and wide.

"I shall send you on a new quest, and this time you must not fail me."

"Of course not, Your Majesty." The commander rose, fresh determination pinching his noble features. I didn't know this man's name, nor did I care. He was only one of many who'd served me and failed. Likely he would fail me again and meet his demise, as had all the others who'd come before him.

"Today you must leave with all haste. And do not return until you find Princess Pearl."

The relief that had moments ago been upon the commander's face fell away, replaced with undisguised dismay. "How are we to find Princess Pearl, Your Majesty, when she is dead?"

I still seethed whenever I realized Pearl had outsmarted me and escaped. Of course, I hadn't comprehended it right away. When the huntsmen had returned with the heart as I'd requested, I'd believed we finally had the ingredient we needed to make gold—the heart of not only the fairest maiden, but also a heart beating with royal blood.

However, the alchemy experiments had failed

completely, and one of my alchemists had discovered the huntsmen had brought in the heart of a deer. Though the huntsmen all denied knowing what had happened to the princess, I'd meted out punishment, killing those privy to my plans and sending the rest to languish as slaves in the mine.

Princess Pearl was not dead. Not in the least. And now it was time to lure her out of hiding, capture her, and finish getting what I needed from her—her heart. I had to do so before time ran out.

"I have received word," I said loud enough to reach the far corners of the great hall. "The princess is alive but has been hiding these many months, raising an army of dangerous dissidents and scheming how she might attack Warwick and take the throne away from me."

I paused, reveling in the gasps and murmurs arising. Of course, I'd heard no such things, but I had to rally the people to my side and not to Pearl's.

"We must find her," I said even louder and with authority, "before she can attack."

"How do you suggest we locate her, Your Majesty?" the commander asked.

I'd been mulling over how to do so all week, analyzing the princess's weaknesses. And after much speculation, I'd figured out exactly what would cause the princess to come out of hiding.

All I had to do was threaten to destroy the one person she cared about most—Ruby. Once I did so, Pearl would cut out her own heart and deliver it to me in order to save her younger sister. Of that I was certain.

Jody Hedlund is the best-selling author of over thirty historicals for both adults and teens and is the winner of numerous awards including the Christy, Carol, and Christian Book Award. She lives in central Michigan with her husband, passel of busy young adults, and five spoiled cats. Learn more at JodyHedlund.com

Young Adult Fiction from Jody Hedlund

The Fairest Maidens

Beholden

Upon the death of her wealthy father, Lady Gabriella is condemned to work in Warwick's gem mine. As she struggles to survive the dangerous conditions, her kindness and beauty shine as brightly as the jewels the slaves excavate. While laboring, Gabriella plots how to avenge her father's death and stop Queen Margery's cruelty.

Beguiled

Princess Pearl flees for her life after her mother, Queen Margery, tries to have her killed during a hunting expedition. Pearl finds refuge on the Isle of Outcasts among criminals and misfits, disguising her face with a veil so no one recognizes her. She lives for the day when she can return to Warwick and rescue her sister, Ruby, from the queen's clutches.

Besotted

Queen Aurora of Mercia has spent her entire life deep in Inglewood Forest, hiding from Warwick's Queen Margery, who seeks her demise. As the time draws near for Aurora to take the throne, she happens upon a handsome woodcutter. Although friendship with outsiders is forbidden and dangerous, she cannot stay away from the charming stranger.

The Lost Princesses

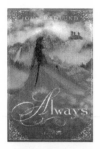

Always: Prequel Novella

On the verge of dying after giving birth to twins, the queen of Mercia pleads with Lady Felicia to save her infant daughters. With the castle overrun by King Ethelwulf's invading army, Lady Felicia vows to do whatever she can to take the newborn princesses and their three-year-old sister to safety, even though it means sacrificing everything she holds dear, possibly her own life.

Evermore

Raised by a noble family, Lady Adelaide has always known she's an orphan. Little does she realize she's one of the lost princesses and the true heir to Mercia's throne . . . until a visitor arrives at her family estate, reveals her birthright as queen, and thrusts her into a quest for the throne whether she's ready or not.

Foremost

Raised in an isolated abbey, Lady Maribel desires nothing more than to become a nun and continue practicing her healing arts. She's carefree and happy with her life . . . until a visitor comes to the abbey and reveals her true identity as one of the lost princesses.

Hereafter

Forced into marriage, Emmeline has one goal—to escape. But Ethelrex takes his marriage vows seriously, including his promise to love and cherish his wife, and he has no intention of letting Emmeline get away. As the battle for the throne rages, will the prince be able to win the battle for Emmeline's heart?

The Noble Knights

The Vow

Young Rosemarie finds herself drawn to Thomas, the son of the nearby baron. But just as her feelings begin to grow, a man carrying the Plague interrupts their hunting party. While in forced isolation, Rosemarie begins to contemplate her future—could it include Thomas? Could he be the perfect man to one day rule beside her and oversee her parents' lands?

An Uncertain Choice

Due to her parents' promise at her birth, Lady Rosemarie has been prepared to become a nun on the day she turns eighteen. Then, shortly before her birthday, a friend of her father's enters the kingdom and proclaims her parents' will left a second choice—if Rosemarie can marry before the eve of her eighteenth year, she will be exempt from the ancient vow.

A Daring Sacrifice

In a reverse twist on the Robin Hood story, a young medieval maiden stands up for the rights of the mistreated, stealing from the rich to give to the poor. All the while, she fights against her cruel uncle who has taken over the land that is rightfully hers.

For Love & Honor

Lady Sabine is harboring a skin blemish, one that if revealed could cause her to be branded as a witch, put her life in danger, and damage her chances of making a good marriage. After all, what nobleman would want to marry a woman so flawed?

A Loyal Heart

When Lady Olivia's castle is besieged, she and her sister are taken captive and held for ransom by her father's enemy, Lord Pitt. Loyalty to family means everything to Olivia. She'll save her sister at any cost and do whatever her father asks—even if that means obeying his order to steal a sacred relic from her captor.

A Worthy Rebel

While fleeing an arranged betrothal to a heartless lord, Lady Isabelle becomes injured and lost. Rescued by a young peasant man, she hides her identity as a noblewoman for fear of reprisal from the peasants who are bitter and angry toward the nobility.

A complete list of my novels can be found at jodyhedlund.com.

Would you like to know when my next book is available? You can sign up for my newsletter, become my friend on Goodreads, like me on Facebook, or follow me on Twitter.

Newsletter: jodyhedlund.com
Goodreads:
goodreads.com/author/show/3358829.Jody_Hedlund
Facebook: facebook.com/AuthorJodyHedlund
Twitter: @JodyHedlund

The more reviews a book has, the more likely other readers are to find it. If you have a minute, please leave a rating or review. I appreciate all reviews, whether positive or negative.

Made in United States
Orlando, FL
09 April 2022